SARAH PURDUE

◆

FINDING ALICE

Complete and Unabridged

LINFORD
Leicester

First published in Great Britain in 2017

First Linford Edition
published 2018

A catalogue record for this book is available
from the British Library.

ISBN 978–1–4448–3814–5

Published by
F. A. Thorpe (Publishing)
Anstey, Leicestershire

Set by Words & Graphics Ltd.
Anstey, Leicestershire
Printed and bound in Great Britain by
T. J. International Ltd., Padstow, Cornwall

This book is printed on acid-free paper

1

Evie Spencer had been sat waiting for hours, but had no intention of leaving. She would wait for the rest of her life if she had to. The problem with sitting and waiting was that her mind whirled with all the possible outcomes, and however hard she tried, she couldn't find a positive one among them. That and the heat. It was a beautiful summer's day outside, perfect for finding a spot in the shade of a café's umbrella and drinking ice cold coffee but not for sitting in an airless, stifling corridor waiting to be seen. The public waiting area in the British Embassy in Rome was surprisingly busy. It seemed that a fair few British tourists had managed to lose their passports, and there was a steady stream of her fellow countrymen who came in looking distressed, but left looking relieved. She fervently wished she

1

could join them.

The click-click of high heels was the first sign that perhaps her wait was over. A tall, willowy woman dressed in chic black walked towards her.

'The Deputy Consul will see you now, Miss Spencer,' the women said, all politeness but with a definite lack of interest.

Evie found her feet and grabbed her rucksack. She knew she looked a state — her long brown hair scraped back into a messy ponytail, and her jeans a few days past needing a wash — but she didn't care. None of that mattered: only Alice mattered.

She followed the woman down a maze of corridors into the heart of the Embassy. Staff bustled about, and everyone seemed to have plenty to do. Evie couldn't imagine any of it was important: her sister was missing, and she knew it was unlikely that any of them were doing anything to help — nobody was. But that was about to change. She wasn't going to be fobbed off with platitudes and weak reassurances any more.

The woman knocked lightly on the door, opened it and ushered Evie inside. The office was elegantly decorated with art and textiles, themed in warm burgundies and mustard yellows. The furniture was all leather and dark wood. An older woman sat behind the desk: Elizabeth Sullivan, Deputy Consul and head of the Embassy staff, junior only to the Ambassador himself. She gestured for Evie to sit.

'Miss Spencer,' the older woman said, removing her glasses and piercing Evie with her gaze. Evie was reminded of being in the headmaster's office at school, but kept her gaze level.

'Let me cut straight to it. Whilst I appreciate your concerns, and have sympathy for them, you cannot harangue Rome's chief of police in the streets. There is a strict protocol to follow.'

Evie opened her mouth to speak, to defend herself, but a warning hand made her keep her peace.

'You must understand, not only does it make it politically difficult for me to assist you in any way, but it also generates a reactive lack of interest in your sister's situation.'

Now Evie couldn't hold her tongue any longer. Her sister's *situation* — that was a step too far.

'My sister has disappeared, without a trace. I wouldn't class that as a *situation*. I would say it is highly likely that she is the victim of foul play, and yet nobody seems to be interested.'

Elizabeth Sullivan picked up her glasses and looked at a buff-coloured file on her desk, the contents of which Evie was unable to see. 'Chief Roberto believes that your sister has gone travelling.'

Evie dug her fingernails into the palm of her hand to prevent herself screaming out loud.

'Alice wouldn't do that. She has worked too hard for too long to earn her place at the Fabrizio School of Art. Why would she just up and leave

4

partway through her first term?'

It was a question that Evie had been asking herself for the eleven days since she last had contact with Alice, and there was no answer that she could think of which would indicate that her sister had chosen to leave.

'It is a very pressured environment. If Alice was struggling, or perhaps it was not what she had hoped it would be . . .' Elizabeth Sullivan's voice trailed off, but Evie could see the hint of something in her face, some small sign that she was unconvinced by her own argument.

'Then she would have told me,' Evie said through clenched teeth. 'My sister and I are very close, and we are in contact every day. I haven't heard a single thing from her for eleven days.' Evie looked at the carriage clock that sat on a dark wooden table surrounded by photographs of the Deputy Consul with famous political and national figures. Eleven days and nine hours, she reminded herself. Alice wouldn't do that to her, whatever the situation, unless she was physically unable. That thought brought the now-familiar fear to the surface and Evie felt bile burn in her throat.

Ms Sullivan stood up from her chair and made her way softly round to the front of the desk.

'I do understand, Miss Spencer, and I will do all that I can. But you must understand the impact that you have when you insult the person who is best placed to help you, particularly in front of his men. There are certain ways of doing things here, and that is not one of them.'

Evie looked up as the older woman reached out and briefly laid a hand on her shoulder.

'Please go back to your hotel and wait. I will update you every day on any news I have.'

Evie swallowed. It was not what she wanted to hear; but a small part of her, the part that was still calm enough to think straight, told her that she was probably right. And even if she wasn't, Evie was wasting time she could be spending searching for her sister. She stood up and held out her hand for the older woman to shake.

'Thank you for your time, Ms Sullivan.' Evie couldn't bring herself to apologise for her behaviour, but she knew she needed to say something. 'I will try to be patient. Please call me the moment you have any news.'

Ms Sullivan held on to her hand for a moment as she studied Evie's face, which she fought to keep neutral.

'Please try, Miss Spencer,' she said before finally letting go of Evie's hand. Evie nodded tightly and then walked quickly to the door, afraid that the little composure she had remaining was about to leave her.

★ ★ ★

As the door closed behind her visitor, Elizabeth Sullivan retook her seat. A door to the left of her desk, which was nearly hidden within the room's panelling, opened.

'Well?' she asked with an eyebrow raised.

Tom De Santis stepped into the room. He wore a dark suit and his hair was cut to military grade. He was tall and broad, and his face displayed no emotion.

'I can see what you mean. I don't think she is going to give up lightly.'

Ms Sullivan leaned back in her chair with her eyes on the now-closed door.

'You know what to do?' she asked, then turned her gaze to him.

'Yes, ma'am,' he said; and then he was gone, making no noise. He had disappeared from the room, and it was as if he had never been there.

Ms Sullivan pushed her glasses back up her nose and turned her attention back to the folder of information on her desk. There was no doubt the situation needed careful handling, but De Santis was the man for the job — of that, Ms Sullivan was certain.

2

Evie stepped through the tall wrought-iron gates that surrounded the Embassy and tried to decide on her next plan of action. Her stomach ached and her legs felt leaden. A sensible person would go and get something to eat, then lie down for a few hours, but Evie knew that as soon as she tried to close her eyes she would replay all the nightmare images of Alice in trouble that seemed to crowd her mind. Instead, she headed left up the main street in the direction of the studios of the Fabrizio Art School, the place that Alice had described to her in exquisite detail and clearly loved.

As she walked, her mind ran through the names of people that Alice had become friendly with. She had already tracked them all down and managed, with her Italian phrase book, to question them about Alice's disappearance. None of them, it seemed, could shed any light and would only give suggestions such as 'Art pilgrimages' which was her rough translation of their words. It was probably pointless to go and ask them the same questions but Evie knew that doing nothing wasn't an option.

She took a lane which led from the street which housed many of the international embassies, heading to the north of the city, renowned for its artistic contingent. As she walked, the streets became quieter away from the tourist centre. The tall buildings with windows and shutters were becoming more worn and uncared for but it was the part of the city that had fired Alice's imagination far more than the famous attractions of Rome proper. Alice had painted her tiny portraits of the places she had loved and sent them to Evie as postcards. Evie swung her rucksack to her right side and reached in to pull out the bundle, which she had carefully wrapped in tissue paper before placing in a clear plastic bag.

When Evie had first arrived, she had retraced Alice's steps as far as possible, using the tiny paintings as indications of where Alice might have gone or been going to, but that had led nowhere other than into a deeper sense of loss and fear. She searched through the collection for her favourite, but couldn't find what she was looking for. Panic started to rise inside her as she wondered if she had lost it, and she felt the tears build up. Her legs felt suddenly weak beneath her and she sat down, hard, on a small step at the front of one of the many worn buildings. It must be here, she told herself firmly, but her hands were shaking so much that all she succeeded in doing was to spill her precious postcards all over the dusty lane. A gentle breeze picked them up, and they danced around her as if they found the whole thing amusing. Evie cried out and started to scrabble around in the dust, reaching for them desperately.

'Here, let me help you,' a voice said as if from nowhere. A voice that even through Evie's ragged mind sounded comfortingly English.

Evie looked up in the face of a man, almost entirely in shadow. She squinted and he knelt in front of her before handing back all the postcards he had rescued.

'Thank you,' she managed to say. She could see his face now: it was politely concerned, but guarded.

'Is everything okay?' he asked

Evie let out a bitter laugh.

'Not even a little bit,' she said before she had realised the words she had spoken. 'But thank you for your help.' She went to stand. What she didn't need right now was a tourist adopting her. She had to focus. She forced her legs to straighten, but as she did so the world started to slide sideways; and she wondered if, to add to everything, she was about to experience her first earthquake.

'Whoa. Careful there!' the man said, and Evie felt arms reach out to steady her. The world stopped its sideways tilt, but black dots continued to dance in front of her eyes, and a small part of her brain tried to remember when she had last eaten something.

'I'm fine,' she said, trying to take a step away, but it seemed that even determination and sheer bloody-mindedness were not going to help her now.

'No, you're not,' the voice said, and this time it was stern. 'There is a small café just around the corner. You can sit in the shade and have something to eat and drink. You look like you need it.'

Evie blinked. Despite the stern, commanding voice, there was compassion there. The genuine sort, not the lip service she felt she had been paid by all in authority up to that point. She had thought it would make the tears return, but instead she found it strangely empowering. She also knew that he was probably right. She would be of little use to Alice if she collapsed and ended up in hospital, especially over something as foolish as failing to eat.

She nodded her agreement. The man kept his hand at her elbow on the short walk, but soon she found herself in a chair outside a small café on a narrow side street.

'Luca!' the man shouted as a young lad appeared wearing dark trousers and shirt and a long white apron from his waist. The man rattled off an order in Italian that was too fast for Evie to even attempt to translate, and as she sat she revised her assessment of him. He was clearly not a tourist more like a regular visitor or even a resident. He was dressed in navy-blue linen trousers and a white linen shirt — which had a pair of sunglasses hooked into the open collar — and had black, closely cropped hair. He looked like he could pass for an Italian, but his English accent suggested that he was from somewhere nearer her home.

Luca reappeared with a silver tray laden with chilled bottles of water and glasses of ice. He placed them in front of Evie, and her companion poured water into the glass before handing it to her.

'Drink,' he urged, and Evie took some grateful gulps as she started to feel the world steady on its axis. Luca returned with coffee and a range of pastries and fruit.

'Eat something.' Again, the man was insistent, and Evie didn't need to be told twice. She felt hungry for the first time since she had arrived. The sugar rushed through her and the fog over her brain seemed to lift.

She became aware that her companion was studying her.

'Thank you for this,' Evie said with a gesture of her hand. 'I've been a little too preoccupied to eat, and I should know better.' She added the last bit with a frown. She had to take better care of herself.

'It's no problem,' the man said, not taking his eyes off Evie even as he drank his coffee.

'Evie Spencer,' she said feeling like she should at least introduce herself to her rescuer, since he seemed to not be inclined to do so.

'Nice to meet you,' he replied, and didn't offer up his name. Evie took a sip of coffee and looked at him carefully. He seemed to realise that he had missed a step, and added, 'Tom De Santis.'

Evie couldn't work out his reluctance to share that most basic piece of personal information. Perhaps he wasn't looking for an attachment any more than she was. Perhaps he was concerned that now he had helped her, he would be stuck with her? Well, she could put his mind at rest there. She took one last sip of coffee and then unzipped the front pocket of her cargo trousers which housed her purse, safe from would-be pickpockets. She pulled out a twenty-euro note. She had no idea how much the coffee and pastries would cost — Rome was eye-wateringly expensive — but figured that would cover it, and would avoid either any uncomfortable attempts to split the bill, or Mr De Santis having to pay the whole cost.

'Thank you for your help, but I must be going.'

De Santis said nothing for a few heart-beats, and Evie thought that she had made her escape. She went to stand, but then felt a hand firmly close over hers.

'You clearly need some assistance, Miss Spencer,' he said, his voice level and unemotional.

'Thank you, but you have already done more than enough.'

De Santis seemed to absorb this comment and consider it.

'You have lost something?' he asked, and when she didn't react he nodded. 'Perhaps I should say, you have lost some*one*?'

Evie could feel her shoulders sag under the weight of those words. It seemed so much worse when spoken out loud.

'If that is the case, then I can help you.'

Evie was torn between asking how or why, but settled for the most urgent question.

'How?' she croaked, 'How can you help me?'

'I am a businessman, Miss Spencer. I

have connections and I speak the language.'

Evie shook her head; it did not add up. Why would he want to help her?

'Why?' she said. 'Why would you want to help me? What's in it for you?' She could feel colour rise in her cheeks. She had not meant to say the last out loud. She looked away from him. Whilst she was embarrassed, she also needed to know. But he said nothing, merely looked at her, and she could not read his thoughts.

'I recognised the signs,' he said finally, so softly that she thought her imagination might be playing tricks on her, saying what she wanted him to say. She looked up at him, but now his gaze was distant, as if in a different place and time.

'I'm sorry,' she said. The words were hollow and she knew it. She wondered how many times people had said that to her, not knowing what else to say. He nodded at her as if he understood what she hadn't spoken.

'I know how the system works, Miss

Spencer. I know how frustrating it can be. I can help you navigate that, if you let me.'

The idea that she might not be in this entirely alone brought hope that Evie thought had died days before, but it did not completely overwhelm her natural caution. Could fate be so kind as to throw exactly the right person into her path, just when she was at her lowest, when she needed it most? That had not been her experience of life before. *Don't look a gift horse in the mouth,* her beloved grandfather's voice seemed to say in her mind. And she smiled at the thought of him using one of his favourite expressions. De Santis looked fleetingly puzzled but said nothing.

'It is a kind offer,' she said, 'but I cannot pay you.' She looked him directly in the eye and saw no reaction to this statement. She hoped that meant that money was not a factor.

'As I said, Miss Spencer, I am a businessman. Money is not my objective.'

'Then what is?'

'I will not force you to accept my help, but merely offer it, with no strings attached. I understand your mistrust.'

Evie opened her mouth to speak, feeling suddenly as if she had insulted him deeply, but he waved her expression away with a hand.

'I appreciate that you may need time to consider my offer. I will be here tonight for my evening meal. If you wish to return and meet with me, we can discuss your situation further. If not, then I promise I will not trouble you again.'

He stood so abruptly that it made Evie jump. He handed her back the twenty-euro note.

'There is no need to pay,' he said, and Evie opened her mouth to argue. 'One of the perks of being the owner.' And then he was gone, striding off towards the main thoroughfare, leaving Evie to try and work out what had just happened.

3

Evie stood outside the doors to the Fabrizio Art School. It had been a frustrating afternoon. Alice's friends and fellow students appeared reluctant to speak with her again, although whether this was because they were annoyed at her repeatedly asking the same questions in broken Italian or because they knew more than they were saying, Evie wasn't sure. What she was certain of was that she was making no progress. She considered going back to the central police station to see if the investigation had progressed at all, but Ms Sullivan's words still echoed in her mind, and she knew that she would be unlikely to keep her temper now any more than she had on her other visits there.

Instead she headed back in the direction of her hotel, wondering how much longer she could afford to stay there, and trying not think about the small café that would be only a slight diversion from her route. Evie shook her head. The real question was: could she trust him? Could she trust Thomas De Santis who had miraculously appeared in her hour of need? And therein lay the problem: she just didn't believe in miracles. Her childhood had relieved her of that burden.

Her mobile phone beeped and she dragged it out of her pocket, trying to push down the hope that it would be a message from Alice, knowing that it would be followed by a wave of bitter disappointment and mounting fear.

Trying to remember to breathe, she dialled her voicemail service.

'Miss Spencer, this is Deputy Consul Elizabeth Sullivan. I have news which is not what we had hoped, I'm afraid.' Evie frowned; she was sure there was no 'we' at this point.

'I have been unable to convince the chief of police to start an active investigation. He feels there is plenty of evidence to suggest that Alice has simply taken a trip. I have, however, convinced him to keep Alice's file open; which means that, should she use her passport to cross any of Italy's borders, he will inform me immediately.'

The voice message continued, but Evie knew that she had heard it all before: warnings to stay away from the police, and empty platitudes about how she expected that Alice would soon turn up, full of youthful enthusiasm and embarrassment at the fuss she had caused.

That was the problem: no one understood her relationship with Alice. What little family they'd had was gone by the time Evie turned nineteen. Since, then it had just been the two of them, and so they were more than just sisters — they were each other's entire family, and they would never put each other through a moment's pain, not if they had a choice.

Evie knew then that she had made up her mind. Whatever Tom De Santis' motive for helping her was, she didn't care — all she cared about was finding Alice. It was a risk, trusting this stranger, she knew that; but she also knew that she would do whatever it took to locate her sister.

When she reached the café, it was full to overflowing. The tables which had simply formed a circle around the open sides now spilled out into the street. People were eating, drinking, and gesturing loudly in Italian. Evie stopped a distance away and scanned the seated patrons for any sign of Tom De Santis, but she couldn't pick him out in the crowd. The young waiter, Luca, appeared and caught sight of her. He nodded and then waved. Evie pushed away the feeling that she might be making a terrible mistake, and forced her legs to move forward.

'Signor De Santis?' he asked with his head to one side. Evie nodded and then followed Luca off the street and into the café, winding their way through the narrow gaps between tables. A few of the patrons passed her a curious glance but were quickly drawn back into their own conversations. They walked behind the bar and down a corridor past the kitchens to an unmarked door. Luca knocked and poked his head inside, speaking in a rush of Italian, then stepped back and gestured to her to enter.

Evie had expected an office of sorts, but the door led outside to a small terraced area. There was a long table and many chairs, but only one was taken.

'Miss Spencer, please have a seat,' Tom De Santis, said standing up. Evie couldn't tell if he had been expecting her to reappear or not; he gave nothing away.

'I wasn't sure if I was going to come,' she said, wondering if she could bait him into revealing more of his motives.

'Neither was I,' was all he said in reply as Luca reappeared with a bottle of red wine and a bowl full of steaming pasta.

Evie opened her mouth to speak, but

De Santis shook his head.

'Since we are in Italy . . . first we eat, then you can tell me about who you are missing.'

Evie looked at the bowl in front of her. It looked delicious and smelled even better but she wasn't sure she could eat. It seemed like every beat that her heart took meant another moment Alice was missing, and she was doing nothing about it. She picked up her fork and tried to will herself. One thing which had become clear was that she needed to follow his rules to get what she needed from him.

A hand reached out for her shoulder. 'Miss Spencer, we will achieve nothing if you fall over from lack of food. I suspect that you have not eaten since we last met?' He raised an eyebrow, and Evie knew there was no point lying. She shook her head.

'Then eat,' he said, and his voice was almost gentle.

Evie did as she was bidden, and had to admit that it was delicious. Rich and creamy with a spicy kick.

'Have you been to Italy before?' De Santis asked, and Evie stared at him before shaking her head. She had no room in her brain for small talk. His eyes seemed to tell her that he understood.

'My grandparents were Italian, although I grew up in England, I always felt like this was my true home,' he said.

Evie nodded to show that she was listening, but was not sure what to say. At least she was finding out a little bit more about the stranger who had promised to help her.

He waited then as if he was expecting her to speak. Evie sighed inwardly: she didn't enjoy talking about herself, and certainly not about personal stuff; but if this was the only way to move the conversation on to more pressing topics, then she would do it.

'Alice and I were raised by our grandfather. He died when I was nineteen and Alice was ten. It's just us now. No other family.' Evie knew she sounded almost robotic, but over the years she had learnt it was best to cut to the chase. It usually avoided more questions.

De Santis had finished his meal and was now sat back in his chair, wineglass in hand. He seemed to take a moment to digest this information. Most people did, Evie thought as she ate another mouthful. It was generally a bit of a conversation stopper.

'Your parents?' he asked. Probably the obvious question, and one that Evie liked to avoid if at all possible.

'Gone,' she said, knowing that she was giving nothing away.

She could feel De Santis' gaze on her, and so she continued to eat, knowing that making eye contact might cause her to share more than she wanted or needed to.

'I'm sorry,' he said simply, and Evie felt some of the tension leave her shoulders. Most people would have asked more questions, unable to ignore their curiosity at her cryptic statement;

but it seemed that De Santis was better at reading people, better at reading her, than most others. She looked up and managed a weak smile, feeling she needed to acknowledge his understanding without providing an invitation for more questions.

'So, it's just been you and Alice. You must be very close.'

Evie swallowed her mouthful and put down her fork. Finally, someone seemed to understand.

'We speak every day, without fail. It's completely out of character, and I know her better than anyone. It's so frustrating when someone who has never even met her tells me that she's probably just gone off travelling.' She couldn't keep the bitterness from her voice. She looked at De Santis, who was continuing to study her closely.

'It seems unlikely,' he conceded, 'from what you have told me. What do you think has happened to her?'

He asked the question as calmly as if he were asking about her favourite ice cream, but Evie felt her throat tighten.

'Nothing good,' she managed to squeeze out before she forced herself to take a deep breath. She needed to stay in control. She couldn't bring herself to voice her fears out loud; it felt as if they might come true if she did.

'You think, for some reason yet unestablished, that Alice's disappearance is at the hands of another, as yet unknown.' De Santis' words were so to the point that Evie blinked and wondered what his own experience of the missing had been. She thought she saw the shadow of some emotion cross his face, but he was too much in control of himself to let it show for long.

'Will you help me?' Evie asked, wondering why she hadn't asked *how* he could help her, but she felt in that moment he had some kind of power to do so. It remained to be seen if he would choose to.

'Of course, Miss Spencer. I have said I would.' He took one more sip of wine and then set down his glass. From somewhere underneath the table he pulled out a laptop.

'Firstly, you must tell me everything you have found out so far.'

Evie nodded.

'And then we will formulate a plan of action.'

4

When Eve finally stopped talking, she knew it was late. The noise from the café had fallen to a low hum, and there were the sounds of the staff clearing tables and setting up for the next day. She had told De Santis absolutely everything, since he had said nothing was too small or irrelevant. She watched as he read through all the notes he had made.

'Do you have the postcards with you?' De Santis asked. Evie was too tired to ask why he wanted them, so merely reached into her bag and handed them over. He took each in turn, carefully studying the painted front. Evie frowned; she had expected him to read the words that Alice had written, to look for some kind of hidden message in the short, excited notes, but instead he seemed transfixed by the details of the tiny paintings.

'These are very good,' he murmured, almost as if he had forgotten she was there. Evie kept her eyes on his face. She had seen that look before. De Santis knew something about art, of that much she was certain. Evie had spent many hours with Alice watching her work be appraised.

'Do you think Alice's painting had something to do with her disappearance?' Evie asked, her voice sounding loud in the quiet.

De Santis looked up at her sharply, and for a fleeting second Evie saw something on his face. Again, it was gone in a heartbeat, but she was sure that whatever it meant, he was hiding something from her.

'No,' he said firmly, then gave a tight smile. 'I'm sorry, I did not mean to give that impression. I was simply captivated by your sister's style. She certainly has talent. Do you mind?'

De Santis pulled out his mobile phone, and Evie nodded but frowned. She said nothing as he carefully took a photograph of each postcard.

Evie knew that she wouldn't be distracted from the clue De Santis seemed to have unwittingly given her. The thought of it made her frown just a little, but then she forced her face into a tired expression — not difficult since she was exhausted. Only one question was on her mind: why would De Santis try and hide something from her? Evie had previously considered what she thought were all the reasons why Alice might have disappeared, and they tended to focus on her age, her tourist status but she had never really considered her art could be a factor. She just couldn't see how it could be a piece in the puzzle. What she needed was some time alone to try and figure it out.

'I think I have taken enough of your time, Mr De Santis.' Evie said as a yawn came unbidden but well timed. Evie pushed back her chair and found her feet. 'Thank you for listening.'

De Santis didn't miss a beat at the sudden change and somehow that made Evie's mind pinch once more. She couldn't help but feel that something about him just did not sit right.

'Of course, you must be exhausted. I will call you a taxi to take you back to your hotel. I don't think you should be out on the streets of Rome, alone at this time.'

Evie nodded, she would have rather walked but she sensed if she argued the point she would only delay her departure. She watched as De Santis called through the door for Luca and then presumably asked him to hail a cab. A returning shout suggested that he had quickly found one.

'May I suggest that you rest tomorrow? I will start my search, contact some people who can assist us. If you leave me your contact details I will let you know as soon as I have any news.'

Evie took a pen from her bag and tore off a scrap of her notepad before scribbling down her hotel details and her mobile number. She handed it back to De Santis.

35

'Could I have my sister's postcards back please? They are very precious to me.' Evie studied his reaction carefully, but all she saw was a sudden realisation that he had failed to give them back — whether it was a genuine reaction or not, she couldn't tell.

He handed them over as if they were worth a million pounds, and Evie carefully rewrapped them in the tissue paper and then plastic bag, before placing them in her rucksack. De Santis gestured for her to follow him back through to the front of the café, and when they arrived the taxi was waiting.

'Thank you once again, Mr De Santis.'

She saw that quick, tight smile again.

'If we are going to be searching for your sister together, may I suggest you call me Tom?'

Evie blinked. Of all the things she had expected him to say, that was not one of them. She nodded dumbly. He opened the taxi door for her and she slid inside. As the taxi made its slow way down the narrow lane, Evie couldn't resist the urge, and twisted in her seat to look back. De Santis was standing in the street watching the taxi go. He held up a hand as if to wave her off, and then turned and walked back into the café.

Evie settled back into her seat and tried to work out what on earth was going on. She couldn't afford to be distracted, however charming and good-looking De Santis was, but neither could she shake the feeling that somehow he was connected to this in some way, she just didn't know how. She also didn't know if he were friend or foe.

★ ★ ★

De Santis stepped back in to the café and made his way through to the back where a narrow staircase led to the apartment upstairs. Once he had closed the door behind him, he picked up the phone and dialled. It rang only twice at the other end, despite the late hour.

'Well?' a women's curt voice asked on the other end of the line.

'Her investigation is pretty thorough,' he mused out loud.

There was a moment's pause.

'I wasn't asking for an assessment of her detective abilities, De Santis. What does she know?'

'Nothing she can draw conclusions from.' His mind replayed the evening's conversation. Evie Spencer was sharp, and he wondered how long it would be before she started to piece the puzzle together.

'Good. You need to keep it that way.'

De Santis bristled at the not-so-hidden accusation. He would do his work as he always had, even when his boss refused to tell him what was going on. That was the job, after all — you followed orders without complaint or question.

'Of course, Ms Sullivan.' He didn't bother to keep the quiet anger that she had questioned his commitment from his voice.

There was another pause, as if Sullivan were considering his answer.

'You need to be in at six tomorrow. The Ambassador has a meeting with the Chinese trade delegation, and I need you to do the final threat assessment.'

'I'll be there,' he said, and hung up the phone.

De Santis paced his small apartment. It wasn't going to be easy to keep Evie engaged, but away from the action. However, he would have to find a way — any way — to keep her out of it, to keep her from discovering whatever it was that Ms Sullivan didn't want her to know. It left a bad taste in his mouth. He didn't like it, but that was his job; and, as always, he was going to do it, whatever the cost.

5

Tom De Santis was dressed in his best suit, and smoothed his tie as he walked away from his first meeting of the day. He had completed the threat assessment and talked the security team through their duties, leaving Holland, his second-in-command, to run the detail. De Santis had complete faith in his team, which meant he could focus on his other job. He glanced at his watch. It was now nine-thirty, and time to ring Evie's hotel. He knew the best way to keep her out of it was to update her regularly on his 'progress'; without that, he wasn't sure what she might decide to do on her own.

He pressed speed-dial 5 on his phone. It rang, but wasn't answered, and De Santis found himself listening to an automated answering service.

'Miss Spencer, it's Tom De Santis.

Just checking in. I don't want to get your hopes up, but I thought you might appreciate an update on what I have set in motion. Please call me back on this number when you have a chance.'

He hung up and frowned. Then he scrolled through his phone again and found the number for her hotel. He dialled, and the phone was answered by what he assumed from the tone of voice was a young female receptionist. De Santis slipped seamlessly into Italian and asked to be put through to Evie's room. He was not exactly shocked to be told that Miss Spencer had left the hotel several hours earlier, but he still cursed himself. He should have known that she wouldn't just accept his help and leave him to it.

He stuck his head round the door to one of the many offices that lined the corridor.

'Jacobs, I'm out. Phone if anything goes awry.'

'Will do, boss.'

A short while later, De Santis stepped

out onto the street. He had shed himself of his best suit and was now dressed more casually in jeans and a pale lemon cotton shirt. He pulled on his sunglasses and knew that he could pass as a tourist amongst the crowds of Rome. Mentally, he reviewed the postcard paintings that he had seen for the first time the night before. The girl had painted some of the sights of Rome. Other cards recorded her copies of great works of art. He planned a route in his head to take in the locations of both, sure that he would find Evie at one of them. He had been too incautious when he had studied them the night before, too impressed with Alice's talent. It had sparked a connection in his brain, one that he suspected Ms Sullivan had not been keen to share. Worse, it was a reaction that Evie, as tired and worn as she had been, had managed to pick up on.

De Santis had picked the most logical, time-efficient route as always, but somehow deep down he had known where she would be. The Borghese Gallery hosted a mass of beautiful artwork and, more importantly, a Caravaggio that Alice had reproduced in miniature.

That was where he found Evie. She was standing as close as the crowd control ropes and security would allow her. One hand held the postcard, and her eyes moved between the original and the tiny copy. The crowds were moving through the long narrow corridor that housed the Caravaggios, but several of them stopped behind Evie, curious as to what she was doing. Evie, for her part, ignored them, lost in her own world of thought and pain.

De Santis scanned the crowds, looking for signs that someone was watching Evie. He had guessed straight away that Sullivan knew more about what had happened to Alice than she had shared, and he could sense there was danger. Danger to Alice, definitely, and it seemed a sensible conclusion that the risk was also shared by Evie, although he didn't know how. A gallery security guard stood nearby, looking as bored as if he were standing in a queue at the local butcher's, but every now and then his eyes flicked in Evie's direction. It could be that he was just doing his job, just keeping a watchful eye on his ancient charges, but there was something about him, something that made the hair on the back of De Santis' neck bristle.

'There you are, sweetheart!' he said, loudly enough for fellow English tourists to turn and smile. He walked over to Evie and swung an arm around her shoulder. He could feel her stiffen beneath his embrace.

'It's me,' he whispered in her ear. 'Just play along.'

Evie swivelled her neck so that she could look up into Tom's face. She hadn't heard him approach, too lost in the painting, trying but failing to find a clue as to where Alice could be.

'What?' she said, wondering what had brought on this sudden, slightly uncomfortable level of affection, but noticing for the first-time Tom's deep hazel eyes.

'You're attracting attention,' he whispered into her ear, pretending to kiss her neck and hoping that the security guard didn't speak English.

'So?' Evie asked. What was his problem? Attracting attention was the least of her worries. She would stand on the top of the Vatican and scream for answers if that would help her find Alice.

'Not here,' he murmured back, and moved to stand in front of her. 'Time for a coffee, darling? I'm starving, and this old thing will still be here when we get back.'

Evie still looked confused, like she was one step behind, but didn't resist when he took hold of her hand and started to casually walk in the direction of the gallery's café.

When De Santis was sure the security guard was no longer watching, he veered off, following signs to a room that held sixteenth-century religious art. Looking over his shoulder, he pushed on a door that said *Solo per il personale*, and pulled Evie inside with him. They were in a service corridor that was empty of all but a few cleaning carts that were waiting for their end-of-day duty.

'What's going on?' Evie asked, both confused and angry. Who did this man think he was?

'Not here. We need to go somewhere safe.'

It was at this point that Evie concluded that her rescuer was slightly unhinged; considering everything else she had to deal with, she didn't have time for this. She pulled her hand out of his and took a step back, intending to bolt back through the door and lose herself in the crowds, but before she could reach the door handle De Santis had manoeuvred his body to block her escape.

'You need to trust me, Evie,' he said, hoping that she would get the message without him having to spell it out here, a place where he could not be certain they were not being overheard.

Evie let out a humourless laugh.

'Why? You are acting crazy and I have no idea why. I don't have the time or inclination to find out, so get out of my way or I will scream my lungs out.'

With her arms folded across her chest, De Santis knew that she would follow through on her threat . . . which would be unfortunate, to say the least.

'You could,' he said mildly. 'But if you do, you will put yourself in grave danger.'

Evie raised an eyebrow, clearly unimpressed with his argument, and her expression told him everything he needed to know. He was going to have to tell her some of what he knew, just enough to convince her to leave with him, and then — well, then he would figure out what to do next.

'Look, I know more than I've told you.'

He watched closely as her eyes went wide and he saw a flicker of distrust and fear. He held out his hands in a 'calm down' gesture.

'I'm not your enemy, Evie. You must believe me. I work for the British government.'

For a moment, he thought he had managed to convince her; but then she threw her head back and let out a loud, piercing scream. He rushed forward and placed a hand firmly over her mouth as he swung her round and grabbed her waist with the other hand. She fought and twisted, desperate to free herself, like a trapped animal. He felt her foot jab at his instep and grunted away the pain, but held on firm. Then, in a moment, she twisted her head and bit down deep into the palm of his hand. This time he couldn't fight the reflex, and his hand flew from her mouth for a split second. He knew he needed to change his tactics. There was no way he was going to be able to get her out of the gallery without her help and so he let her go.

6

De Santis couldn't help but be impressed by her reflexes; clearly she had previously done some sort of self-defence training as she was at the door in a heartbeat, yanking it open and running back in the direction they had come from. He let her get ahead, and then followed at a slow jog, keeping her in view.

Evie made her way back to the Caravaggio gallery, weaving in and out of the crowds. People were turning to stare at her, and so she forced herself to slow to a fast walk. Garnering this much attention would make her escape route clear to De Santis, and she knew she didn't have long to make her getaway. Her mind raced as she considered her options: she would have to abandon her hotel room, it would be the first place he would look, but at least she'd had the sense to bring her money and her passport with her. She would just have to manage without everything else.

Evie found herself at the wide entrance hall and hurried down the steps. The street was bustling with people, and the traffic flowed with much sounding of horns, the way it did in Italy. Evie risked a glance over her shoulder and saw De Santis leaping down the steps two at a time, calling her name. Without delay, she launched into a run, only to find her arm grabbed by a man who swung her around and used her momentum to send her in the direction of a dark SUV that was parked at the kerb. Her mind raced, wondering if she was about to be mugged, of all things. She was holding out her hands to prevent herself from colliding with the side of the car, but the door opened at the last minute and other hands grabbed for her.

Without time to think, she brought up an elbow and it crunched into the face of the owner of the hands. She didn't have time to stop herself moving forward, and caught her forehead on the door catch. She felt no pain, just a rush of adrenaline. Ducking low so the man who had originally captured her had to realign his grip, she swung out a leg which connected with his ankle. He didn't fall so much as alter his direction, but it was enough for her to take a step away. And now she screamed as she had been taught, and knew that she was drawing attention that the man didn't want. She glared into his eyes, his face now close to hers, and she felt a hand grip her arm and yank her away from him. She brought up her open palm to hit out but it was blocked by an arm.

De Santis said nothing, just hauled her to her feet and dragged her away. Evie risked another glance over her shoulder. Her captor had now climbed back into the SUV and it was speeding away in another direction.

'What?' she managed to say between

sucking air back into her lungs. De Santis said nothing but kept dragging her. Evie could hear sirens in the distance.

'Shouldn't we wait and speak to the police?' she said, leaning back on his grip to slow him down a little. De Santis turned and his eyes flashed with anger.

'Trust me, that's the last thing you want.'

And then Evie was being pulled along — to where, she had no idea.

De Santis had a car parked nearby, but he ignored it. He couldn't be certain if they knew his plates, and it wasn't worth the risk.

'We need to get off the streets.' He said the words aloud, but really they were for his own benefit.

'The café?' Evie asked between breaths.

De Santis shook his head.

'First place they'll look.' The Embassy was the obvious choice, but that would raise too many questions. He tightened his grip on Evie's hand. He had an idea, but they had to be fast.

Evie had no idea where they were. They had been down so many side streets and winding lanes that she couldn't be certain that she wasn't being dragged in circles. She had no idea what she should do; and so for want of a better idea she continued to follow De Santis, and didn't make a fuss when they passed other pedestrians. Right now, she had no idea who to trust, but something told her making a break for it on her own would be a mistake. Clearly De Santis knew more about Alice's disappearance than he had let on, and there was no way Evie was going to let him out of her sight until he had told her everything.

De Santis' pace slowed, and Evie wondered if all the running was finally making him breathless, but his breathing remained slow and steady. The noise of a moped behind them made him spin on the spot, and then Evie found herself shoved bodily through a window which De Santis had levered upwards. Her landing was soft, if not particularly elegant, and she shifted in time to avoid being squashed by De Santis who dived through the window to land next to her. She opened her mouth to speak and found herself once again with his hand firmly over her mouth. She glared at him, but the noise of footsteps outside the window made her freeze.

De Santis flashed his eyes in warning, but he needn't have bothered: Evie's face showed that she understood. Slowly, he took his hand away, and reached up silently to flick the latch before he wriggled back down beside her. The window rattled above them, but the latch held. After what felt like an age, the footsteps moved further away, and there was the sound of the small engine turning over. Evie waited a few moments more, just to be sure that whoever was following them — if they had even been following them — had gone.

'Okay. Now is the time that you tell me what the hell is going on.'

De Santis seemed to ignore her as he got to his feet and walked to the door to the basement. He cricked it open and did a quick sweep of whatever was on the other side. He seemed satisfied as he pulled the door and slid across the bolt.

'It's not The Ritz, but it should do,' he said as his mind whirled to form some sort of plan — the first part of which was to find out who was involved in whatever this was, and why they wanted Evie.

'It will do for what?' Evie asked, and there was no mistaking the dangerous tone in her voice.

'As a safe house. For you,' De Santis said, finally turning his attention back to her. Her cheeks were flushed with the effort of running through the heat, and her hair had fallen half out of its tight, businesslike bun — it suited her better like this, he thought, and then immediately banished the thought from his head. He didn't have time, although he couldn't help but be impressed with how she handled herself.

'I don't think so,' Evie said, and stood up, taking a step towards the door and wondering if she was going to have to repeat her screaming performance for another time today.

'Don't bother,' De Santis said, as if he could read her mind. 'This district is pretty much deserted, and these walls — ' He used his fist to thump one of the thick stone sides of the basement. ' — are pretty much soundproof.'

'Are you telling me that I've just been kidnapped?' Evie said, unable to keep the scepticism from her voice. This could not be happening. She was supposed to be rescuing Alice from wherever she was, not getting taken herself.

'Of course not,' De Santis said, and he looked as if he had just been badly insulted.

'Fine,' Evie said. 'Then stand away from the door and let me go. If you do, I promise I won't go to the police.'

'Trust me, they won't help you,' De Santis said, wondering what he needed to say to make her understand.

Evie raised an eyebrow.

'Why? Because you have them in your pocket? Have you bought them out so they won't investigate you for whatever it is you're up to? Businessman? Really? Is that what they're calling it these days?'

De Santis had to bite back a laugh, Evie certainly had spirit.

'Miss Spencer . . . ' he started.

'If you're going to hold me against my will, you can at least call me Eve or Evie.'

De Santis blinked. Again she had managed to surprise him.

'Eve,' he started slowly, 'I'm only going to hold you against your will if you don't agree to stay here, where it's safe.'

Evie folded her arms.

'Safe from what, exactly?'

'Safe from the men who, not an hour ago, tried to bundle you into a car,' he said mildly. Again, he had to hide a smile as he saw her remember the recent event.

'Who were they?'

'I have no idea,' De Santis said. 'But they seemed to want you, and I doubt they were just offering to take you on a free tour of the sights.'

'This has something to do with Alice?'

'I would imagine so,' he answered and pulled out his mobile, frowning at the lack of signal. When he looked up he saw a small smile on Evie's face. That was not the reaction he was looking for: scared and compliant would have been easier.

'So, I must be getting close.' She looked at De Santis closely, checking for a reaction, 'I mean, to come after to me in broad daylight. That's pretty rash.'

De Santis crossed the room and caught hold of both of her arms. He needed her to understand just how serious, just how dangerous, the situation was.

'Eve. The very fact that they would come after you in broad daylight is the reason you should be afraid. Whatever Alice is mixed up in, it involves serious people. People who believe they are above the law. Do you understand?'

Evie nodded, but De Santis knew that he was fighting a losing battle.

'I can help you, but only if you do as I say. I can't find Alice if I'm worried about you.'

Evie looked up sharply, but De Santis' expression appeared genuine.

'You don't need to worry about me. I'm not your responsibility.' She held his gaze, 'But Alice is mine. And I will do anything I can to get her back safe.'

'Anything except listen to the guy trying to help you?'

Evie turned away from him and walked across the empty basement to where a shaft of light made it through the grimy street-level window.

'How do I know that you aren't involved?'

Evie turned, determined to look for any fleeting expression that might betray his real motives, but all she saw was the door being pulled to and the sound of a key turning in the lock.

7

Evie had tried everything. She had hammered on the door for what felt like hours. She had yelled and screamed. She had tried the small window that had been her entrance into this prison, but De Santis must have found something to jam it shut from the outside. Evie had paced the room with her mobile, desperately trying to get a phone signal, although she wasn't certain who she would call if she found one. It was clear that no one was who they said they were, and no one could be trusted. Having tried everything she could think of, she sat down. Conserving her strength would be important, especially since she had no idea how long De Santis would keep her locked up.

The key rattled in the lock, and Evie scrabbled to her feet and rushed to the door, hoping to take the person by surprise. The door opened just enough for a plastic bag to be tossed through.

'I brought you water and some food.' De Santis' voice seemed to echo around the empty room, and seemed painfully loud after hours of near silence. 'Step away from the door. I have a blanket and a torch.'

Evie took a step back, but with no intention of following his instructions. She braced her legs, and when he stepped through the door she ran straight at him, hoping that her forward momentum would be enough to at least cause him to stumble; but he had anticipated her move, and instead her momentum was used against her. She found herself pulled round and held firmly against his body.

'Do you ever follow instructions?' he asked, sounding faintly amused.

Evie wriggled, testing his grip. She wasn't going to waste her energy arguing with the man who had kidnapped her. She felt him shift his weight and kick the door closed, and then he released his grip.

'I can tell what I've found out, but you'll have to stop fighting.' He raised an eyebrow and Evie backed up against the wall. It was about the only reason that would persuade her to temporarily stop trying to escape. She gestured with her hand to show that he should continue. De Santis remained in position, standing between her and the only exit. To an untrained eye, it might look as if he had dropped his guard, but Evie recognised the stance. If she tried anything, he would be ready.

'I have been in touch with a contact at Europol.'

Evie raised an eyebrow. She would never tell him that she was impressed, not after all that he had done . . . but she was, just a little. De Santis seemed satisfied with her reaction and so continued.

'I gave a description of the guy that tried to grab you, and they found a match. A relatively low-level goon in organised crime.'

Evie stared, now starting to wonder if he was just spinning her a tale.

'The Mafia? Seriously? You don't expect me to believe that! We aren't starring in some Hollywood block-buster.'

De Santis just looked at her, his expression neutral. Evie replayed the events outside the gallery and had to admit that, with even her limited knowledge, it did seem a little mob-like. She just couldn't believe it was happening to her.

'So why Alice?' she asked, trying to swallow down the lump of emotion that had appeared in her throat. 'What do they want with her?' She managed to say the words although a part of her didn't want to ask, didn't want to know.

De Santis took a step towards her and she stayed where she was. However much she wanted to, she wasn't going to back away from this.

'Her art,' he said simply, and Evie frowned; she had been thinking there had to be a connection, but she couldn't for the life of her figure out what.

'What, some mob boss likes her art so much that they kidnapped her?'

De Santis shook his head. 'It's organised crime, not some romantic take on mob life. Organised crime is about power, and power is all about money.'

Evie shook her head. 'Then what?'

De Santis took a deep breath, and for a moment Evie thought he was going to refuse to say whatever it was that he was keeping from her.

'The idea came to me when I saw the postcards. They were just quick sketches, but they were good copies — not just in appearance but in method.'

'And what would you know about that?' Evie asked as her brain started to fix the pieces of the puzzle together.

'I'm just an amateur, but I showed the photos I took to a friend of mine who is an expert, and he was impressed. That's when the pieces started to fall into place.'

Tom had to turn away from her then.

There was something about her that made him want to tell her the truth — that he had been assigned to keep her out of this, whatever this was — but he knew he couldn't. It wasn't a choice, it was simply his job, whether he liked it or not. He took a moment to compose himself, clenching and unclenching his fists. He had told her too much already.

He glanced around the room. Still, could it hurt if she was safely away from the action? What he needed right now was for her to trust him. If he could convince her of that, it would make keeping her here easier, and maybe soothe some of the unexpected guilt he was feeling. He could understand her passion to do something — in fact, he respected it — but he couldn't let her get involved, Sullivan's instructions had been clear. Having made up his mind, he turned back to face her.

Evie waited, trying to be patient whilst Tom dealt with whatever internal battle was raging inside him. Despite all her instincts to not be taken in, she had to admit that his story was plausible, if unlikely. But then they weren't in some Hollywood high-octane spy thriller. She crossed her arms and raised an eyebrow as he turned around. She didn't want to give the impression that it was alright for him to kidnap her.

'The pieces?' she said in an arch tone. She knew she was probably being unfair. It did appear as if he was trying to help her, to help Alice, but Evie couldn't shake the mistrust. It had been her constant companion as early as she could remember. People couldn't be trusted, and you shouldn't give them the chance, because such chances inevitably led to pain.

Tom shrugged and Evie felt her anger flare.

'It's just a theory, Eve. I have no proof.'

'Okay.' Evie forced herself to hold her tongue. She wanted to demand answers, but couldn't help but feel that the more she talked, the less Tom would say.

She watched as he ran his hand

through his close-cropped hair, leaving it unruffled.

'As I said, I wonder if Alice's artistic talents have drawn unwanted attention.'

Now it was Evie's turn to move away from him. She needed space to think. It couldn't be that, could it? Surely that sort of thing only happened in novels and movies.

'Are you saying that Alice is involved in forging art?'

8

'Alice would never do that!' Evie said. The very idea that Alice would be involved in anything criminal was laughable. As a child, Alice had once walked out of a shop without paying, with sweets in her hand — completely by accident, but she had cried for days, and even the shop owner had been required to comfort her.

'I'm not suggesting that she would help willingly, Eve. She likely has no choice.'

Evie felt her legs wobble beneath her. The gut-wrenching fear was back, and its constant companion, fatigue, was there too. She reached a hand out for the wall and steadied herself before her body had other ideas and she found herself sat down. Tom stepped towards her and threw a blanket around her shoulders. Wordlessly, he handed her a bottle of water, before drawing a flask out of the bag he had brought with him.

'I didn't mean to upset you,' he said, and Evie could detect nothing other than genuine concern in his voice. She let out a sad laugh.

'You didn't, merely confirmed one of my darkest fears. I knew that Alice wouldn't just up and leave, not if she had the choice.'

'It's just a theory. I have no real proof.'

Evie managed a weak smile.

'But you're the first person to really listen to me and to take my concerns seriously.'

Evie felt Tom settle into a spot beside her on the floor; close, but not so close that they touched. Unbidden, she wished that he would throw an arm around her and tell her that everything would be alright. She almost laughed at her own foolishness. There were only two people in the world that Evie had ever truly trusted: one was her grandfather who had died, and the other was Alice who was goodness knew where. The loneliness was familiar, almost like a blanket, but for the first time in an age Evie longed for someone else to step in and utter those words.

'Look, it's a theory that I can work with . . . ' Tom started.

'I think you mean 'we',' Evie said firmly.

Now Tom raised an eyebrow.

'This is my job, and I work best alone.'

'So, you're not a businessman, then?'

Tom frowned.

'I told you, I work for the British government.'

'You also told me that you were a businessman.' Evie knew that there were more important things to talk about, but couldn't help but try to push this man's buttons. She didn't completely trust him, of course, but she wondered if she could press him to reveal more than he obviously intended to. Tom's face remained smooth, and if anything, Evie wondered if there was some amusement there — whether at her attempts to rile him or something else, she wasn't sure.

'I can't be both?' he asked with an innocent air. Evie shrugged.

'Everything I have told you is the truth,' he started, but stopped when Evie let out a snort.

'Sorry but that seems pretty doubtful.' She waved her hands around to indicate where she was.

'I work for the government and I have business interests in Italy,' he said, keeping his voice as even as if Evie had simply asked him a question. 'My grandparents left them to me, and as I said earlier, I feel more at home here. I have connections that I can use — that I *will* use — to find your sister, but you need to listen to me.'

Evie nodded, not sure whether she was agreeing with him or not, but it seemed like the right thing to do.

'My investigations need to be low-key and kept off the radar of local law enforcement.' Not to mention, out of sight of Sullivan.

Evie wanted to question his mistrust of the locals, but decided that she could think about that later. Right now, she needed to listen to what he had to say.

'In order to do that, I need you out of the way.'

Evie opened her mouth to argue but was hushed by the stopping motion he made with his hand.

'Your presence, as an obvious tourist, brings unwanted attention. Attention that could heighten the risk to Alice.'

Evie's face blanched. The idea that what she had been doing might somehow put Alice in more danger had not been something she had even considered. Her approach had been to make as much noise, as much fuss, as possible . . . but what if she had been wrong? She felt hot tears collect at the corners of her eyes, and did nothing to stop their slow path down her cheeks.

'I'm sorry, Evie, but this is how it needs to be for now. I'll come back when I have some news.'

Evie was barely aware that he had left her side, or that the door to her prison had once again been locked. All she could think of was that her actions might have put Alice in even more danger, and that was a thought that she couldn't bear. She pulled the blanket tightly around herself and curled into a ball. For the first time since Alice had disappeared, she let the emotions flow without any effort to hold them back, and cried herself to sleep.

She woke up cold and stiff. She stood up to get the blood flowing to her freezing feet and tried to organise her thoughts. Despite all the swirling questions in her mind, she focused in on two of them. Firstly, how was she going to get out of her supposed 'safe house'? And secondly, could she trust Tom De Santis? Unfortunately, focusing on these two questions did not give her any immediate answers. The desire to trust Tom was not one that she wanted to encourage. She had trusted people before, and they had almost always let her down. An image of him popped into her mind, as did the sense that she wished he would pull her into his arms and tell her that everything was going to be alright. With some effort, she forced her mind to concentrate on the all-too-familiar mantra: *You can't trust anyone.*

Evie knew the emotions that went with that desire were dangerous. Not only to herself, but also to Alice. Through the tiny window she could see that the sun was rising, but with the thick walls of the basement, it seemed that its heat would not be felt for many hours. As she paced up and down, she came to a decision. She wasn't going to trust Tom De Santis. There were plenty of reasons not to — for one thing, he had not been honest with her from the start, assuming that what he said about working for the British government was even true. But she had a strong sense that he was involved in the whole mess somehow, and so maybe she could use him to find Alice.

Having come to a decision, she felt more positive, and moved towards the bag of food. What she couldn't do was play the damsel in distress, at least not for real. She needed to take care of herself, as she had always done, and that meant eating something. In the bag she found pastries, bottles of water, and chocolate bars. Not exactly a balanced diet, but it would at least give her energy. Taking a bite of pastry, she retraced her steps around her prison, looking for any weak spots that she might be able to escape through. As with her previous circuits, though, she knew she was unlikely to find anything. What she needed to do was wait and work out what she was going to do the next time the door opened.

When it did, Evie was ready. She stood on the other side of the door, so that when it opened, it would appear that the room was empty. She doubted that Tom DeSantis would be thrown by this, but it was all she had been able to come up with.

At the first sound of footsteps, Evie made her way as silently as possible to stand behind where the door would open. There was the sound of keys and then the lock turning.

The door opened slowly. Evie listened as the footsteps faltered, then the door was thrown wide open and Luca came into the room. He was looking around wildly when Evie ran forward and shoved him hard. He sprawled across the floor with the unexpected force, and Evie had to fight the urge to apologise and help him to his feet. Instead, she ran, through the open door and out into the corridor. She could hear shouts behind her in Italian. The voice sounded dismayed — again, Evie felt sorry for him, for she doubted that Tom would be impressed that he had managed to lose her so easily, but she couldn't worry about that right now. One word drove her onwards: *Alice*.

Evie raced down a corridor that split in two. She had no idea of the layout of the building since she had come in through the small window. She took the left-hand branch on a whim, feeling the need to keep moving, and found herself faced with a heavy wooden door that was locked. She cursed under her breath and spun on the spot. She ran back to where the corridor had forked and took the other branch, nearly squealing with relief when she found a set of stone steps. Evie took them two at a time and found herself in what had once been a grand entrance hall but was now crumbling with age.

A double door was in front of her, and she wondered again if it was locked; but the shouts in Italian were drawing closer and she knew she had to make a choice. She ran towards the door and tugged on the heavy iron catch. At first nothing happened, then she felt it give a little. Planting her feet firmly, she yanked hard, and the catch gave some more. The door itself was heavy and swollen with age and weathering, and it made a loud grinding noise as Evie dragged it across the dusty floor. She heard running footsteps on the stairs and tried to work out if the gap was now wide enough for her to squeeze through. The footsteps were on her level now, so she knew she had no more time. She wriggled herself through the gap, a pocket of her trousers catching on a rusty nail. She pulled herself through, ignoring the ripping of material, and ran back in the direction she had been led the day before.

9

Now that she was free, she needed a plan. When she reached a more populated area she forced herself to slow to a walk. Running would only attract attention, and that was the last thing she needed right now. A few stares made her glance down, and she realised that not only did she look like she needed a shower, but she had ripped a huge hole in the leg of her trousers and was showing more of her underwear than could be consider decent. She slipped a hand into her torn pocket and grabbed hold of the flapping material. It wasn't much, but it made her look slightly less like she was the victim of something.

She didn't think she should risk going back to the hotel, but where else could she get a shower and a change of clothes? As she moved between the bustling people who had somewhere to be, and the tourists who seemed to have all the time in the world, she decided to make her way to near the hotel and watch it for a while. If she saw no sign of anyone suspicious, then she would risk going in to collect her belongs. It wasn't much of a plan but she needed to start somewhere.

Evie tried to act like a tourist, using opportunities to stop and stare at a beautiful piece of architecture to check for signs that she wasn't being followed. The streets were teeming with people and Evie suspected that anyone following her would have more experience in the art than what she knew from watching television. Nearing the hotel, she found a spot to stand and watch, around the corner from a pavement café that was busy with customers. She was in the shadows and was fairly certain that no one would spot her. Glancing at the church clock tower, she decided she would watch for an hour, and then if she saw nothing she would approach.

Every second seemed to tick by at the rate of an hour. Evie felt a sense of urgency; several times she nearly gave up and walked across the street, but something was holding her back. She had been incautious before, and Tom had suggested that she might have put Alice in more danger. It might have been a tactic of course, to keep her out of things, but there was an element of truth to it that Evie could not ignore.

Cars came and went. Some pulled up outside the hotel and spilled out businessmen and women and foreign tourists. None looked out of place to Evie's untrained eye. I'll walk over after the next car drives off, she promised herself, not understanding her reluctance after being desperate to move for so long. A taxi pulled up and the driver got out and opened the passenger door. An impossibly elegant woman slipped out as if moving in a short, tight skirt were the easiest thing in the world. She wore sunglasses and carried a dark leather briefcase. The woman tipped the driver and turned to walk up the front steps of the hotel. Evie took a step forward, and then felt a hand clamp over her mouth. Before she could say or do anything, she found herself being pulled back in to the alley.

Within a split second her brain processed what was happening, then she was fighting, twisting her body and trying to inflict some pain on her assailant that might make him loosen his grip, but her efforts seemed to have no effect.

'Easy, tiger.'

The words in her ear were so English that she paused in her struggle just for a moment.

'It's me, Tom. Can you stop the wildcat act for a few seconds and listen to me?'

He loosened his grip enough for Evie to turn her head so she could see it was him.

'Please?' he said in response to her angry glare.

Evie forced her body to obey her and

relax. Tom removed his hand from her mouth, but still had a firm grip on her arm.

'Do you mind telling me what you're doing?' he asked. For a split second all Evie could do was stare at the ridiculous question.

'What does it look like?' The words came out louder than she intended, and the pressure on her arm forced her to take a few more steps into the alley and away from all the people.

'It looks like voluntary stupidity.' His voice was sarcastic but even. 'Or was your plan just to walk in there and let them take you?'

Evie blinked. Was her trying to frighten her, or was he right? She frowned and turned her glare away from him. It seemed Tom had the ability to make her feel like a bumbling idiot at every turn — which, of course, she probably was from his perspective, if he really was an agent for the British government.

'Are you telling me that they would try and take me from my hotel, in broad daylight?' Evie suspected she knew the answer to that question, but felt like she needed to push back a little.

'They tried to take you from Rome's most famous art gallery. What do you think?'

'Who are 'they'?' Evie asked, deciding it was time to move the conversation away from her apparently foolish choices. Tom froze for a split second, but it was so fleeting that Evie couldn't be sure she hadn't imagined it.

'I don't know,' he said, and Evie had no idea if he was telling the truth or not. She said nothing, hoping that her eyes fixed on him might guilt him into saying more, but he just held her gaze, his face carefully neutral.

'I'm not sure this is the way to find out, though,' he added finally, and Evie suspected he was right.

'But if they took me,' she said suddenly as the thought came into her head, 'wouldn't it make it easier to track Alice?'

'You're assuming they would hold

you in the same place. Unlikely. More likely, they would use you to threaten your sister.'

Evie felt a chill run through her. She wasn't worried about herself — she couldn't seem to find that emotion — but she wouldn't make Alice feel any more scared or hurt than she currently was.

'So, what so we do?'

'Again, with the 'we',' Tom said and Evie got the impression that she was managing to try his patience despite his outward appearance of calm.

'Well, I'm assuming the plan isn't for me to stay in this alley and hide until you find Alice.' Evie's voice sounded grumpy in her ears, and again she wondered if she saw a glimmer of amusement in his face.

'You haven't given me much choice. It seems that I can't let you out of my sight. So you're coming with me.'

The grip on Evie's arm loosened and in that moment, she contemplated making a run for it but a small part of herself, a nagging part was wondering if Tom was right. Perhaps he was trying to scare her, but maybe he was concerned that her running around trying to find Alice was going to hinder his investigations. She felt his hand pick up hers, and his face was a question. She wondered, if she said no, whether he would let her go, but instead found herself nodding. With so much at stake she would go with him for now, but she dug the nails of her free hand into her palm to remind herself that she didn't trust him, she *wouldn't* trust him.

'Where are we?' Evie asked looking up. They were standing outside a three-storey building of classical Roman architecture. Unlike the previous 'safe house' this one looked positively palatial. The large door to the building led in to a marble-floored reception and a man in uniform sat at the desk. He nodded to Tom as they walked past him, and Tom led her to a winding marble staircase. They walked up to the top floor in silence. Tom offered no explanation, and Evie got the distinct impression that he wouldn't answer anything whilst they were out in the open.

At the top of the stairs there was only one door, and Tom took out a key and unlocked it. He held the door open for Evie and she walked in. The inside was so much more than the outside that she her mouth fall open in surprise. It was the kind of apartment that you saw on the television, usually associated with millionaires or celebrities. It had clearly been furnished by an expert; everywhere was smooth lines and simplicity that screamed 'expensive'. Evie heard the door close behind her, and the beep of a security system that was quickly silenced.

Evie walked across the open-plan living space to a wall of glass that led out to a balcony that seemed to run halfway around the building. The views of Rome were spectacular.

'Where are we?' Evie asked again. 'Who owns this place?' Her mind was going back once again to the cellar of the derelict building she had spent the night in.

'It's my place, and so strictly against the rules to bring you here.'

Evie turned to face him. He didn't look upset and just shrugged, making Evie wonder if he made a habit of breaking these rules.

'Whose rules?' she asked.

'Mine,' he said, and walked towards the kitchen area, which was all sleek black granite and white fixtures. 'And technically the British government's,' he added, as if that were an afterthought and not really that important.

'Will you get in trouble?' Evie asked, feeling for the first time slightly guilty that she had been giving him such a hard time when it would appear all he was trying to do was help her. Tom shrugged and pulled a bottle of red wine from a well-stacked wine rack.

'It wouldn't be the first time.' Evie watched as Tom pulled two wineglasses from a glass-fronted cabinet and poured two generous servings. He looked up.

'I have soft drink if you prefer?'

Evie shook her head; if nothing else, she figured she deserved a glass of wine. She walked over and took a sip as Tom pulled olives and assorted dips from the fridge.

'Probably a good idea to eat something. It will take me a while to get dinner ready.'

'You cook as well?' Evie said before her brain could process what she was saying. She pursed her lips and tried to pushed down the sense of growing embarrassment that she knew was making her face go red.

'I spent every summer here with my grandparents. They worked in the restaurant all hours, and so I did too. I picked up a few things,' he said, and for the first time he grinned. Evie tried not to admit it to herself, but it suited him. The smile made him look younger and took away the hard edge that seemed to underscore his features. She felt that, perhaps for the first time, she was seeing the real Tom, the one he had kept carefully hidden.

'You cook?' he asked as he started to chop vegetables. Evie coughed as she took a sip of wine at the same time the question registered. Tom looked up but made no move, just waited for her to compose herself.

'Depends who you ask,' Evie said, squashing down the memory that replayed of Alice buying her yet another cookbook — in a desperate attempt, she said, to have something edible to eat.

'Oh?'

'Alice would say I'm a lost cause.' As soon as the words were out of her mouth Evie felt pain overwhelm her. The words she had spoken without thought caused the hope inside her to shrink a little more. 'Lost cause' was one of Alice's favourite expressions, and she could see her sister dancing around the kitchen, pretending to have food poisoning, having tasted one of Evie's latest creations.

'What if I never see her again?' The

words tumbled out of her mouth and were closely followed by a wail. Evie lifted a hand to her mouth, trying to regain control. This was not what she did. She creased her face up and tried to breathe, but the tears would not be held back. And before she knew it she had been pulled firmly into the arms that she had so desperately wanted to hold her.

10

Being held so tightly was unfamiliar to Evie, but she knew that it was what she needed. Her mind seemed to quiet with the sensation, and there was an unfamiliar sense that she was safe. Tom said nothing, just held her and let her cry. Evie wondered if he was breaking another rule of either his or his employers. The thought made her tell herself to get a grip. Gently, she took a step backwards, and wiped a hand across her face.

'Sorry, I don't know where that came from,' Evie said, feeling the need to dispel any ideas Tom might have that she was a damsel in distress.

'No need,' he said simply, before returning to prepare dinner. 'I'm surprised it hasn't happened sooner.'

'Do you get a lot of women falling into your arms in your line of work?'

Evie said, and then winced — that had come out as rather spiteful, and not as she had intended. 'Sorry,' she added once again. She risked a look up, but Tom was focused on throwing his chopped ingredients into a pan, and only the tug of a grin on his face showed that he had heard her.

'Not often, no,' he said when he realised that Evie was looking at him. 'Occasionally my boss has a bad day, and then she needs to have a bit of an encouraging hug.' His grin spread; Evie felt pulled in by it, and returned it without having to fake it.

'Would that be the Ice Queen that I've had dealings with?'

Tom raised an eyebrow.

'She's not an easy person, I know, but that's what makes her good at her job.' There was no sign of it, but Evie wondered if she had somehow just indirectly insulted him.

'Sorry . . . ' she began, but Tom waved her comment away with his hand.

'You apologise a lot, but it's not necessary.'

Evie opened her mouth to speak, then realised that she was going to say sorry again, and closed it.

'Force of habit,' she said ruefully; it was another thing that Alice had teased her about, but then Alice had been mostly sheltered from the upbringing she had experienced at the hands of their overly critical parents.

Tom took his eyes off the pan to look at her, and she felt like he was able to see right into her mind. He nodded, as if he somehow understood what had not been spoken out loud.

'What do you do for a living?' Tom asked, and Evie felt relief that the subject had been changed. With Alice in danger, there was no way she could talk about the painful subject of her parents.

'I work in insurance,' Evie said, and felt the usual faint embarrassment at having such a mundane job.

'Interesting,' Tom said, but there was no trace of derision in his voice.

'Not really, but I needed to get into a secure job quickly. My grandad only had his pension, and I needed to be able to pay something towards the rent and all that other stuff.'

'That must have been tough at nineteen,' Tom said, as a statement rather than a question. Now it was Evie's time to shrug.

'It was easier than the previous eighteen years. And I wanted Alice to have some of the things I didn't.'

'Like the opportunity to pursue her art?' Tom asked, and Evie nodded. She felt the emotion there, but this time she held it in place.

'She's so talented, she deserves every opportunity I can give her — not to mention how hard she has worked.'

'So, if you weren't in insurance, what would you do?'

Evie blinked. It was a question that she never gave herself the luxury to ask, and certainly nothing that anyone else ever asked her — except for Alice, of course.

'I don't know,' she answered honestly, 'I haven't really every thought about it. My job pays pretty well.'

Tom nodded as if he understood the importance of that as he placed cutlery on the breakfast bar in the kitchen and gestured for her to sit.

'Maybe once this is over you should give that some thought.'

Evie took a fork to the risotto that Tom had placed in front of her. Right now, she couldn't imagine this being over. Not that she didn't think about what she would do when Alice was back in her arms, she just couldn't imagine how they would get from where they were right now to that point.

When they had finished eating and Tom had cleared up — Evie had offered to help, but had been refused — Tom showed her around the apartment. There were two bedrooms next to each other. One was obviously the master and had an en-suite attached; it was painted in tones of grey and black, and was clearly Tom's room.

Next to it was a guest room in creams and browns. A king-size bed and widescreen TV made it feel like an exclusive hotel room.

'This is you,' Tom said. 'Bathroom's across the hall. I'll pick you up some clothes and things tomorrow.' He handed her one of his t-shirts. 'You'll find toiletries in the vanity above the sink.'

Evie stared just a little. Somehow, Tom didn't come across as the type of person who would think of such things, being more of a man of action. He chuckled.

'I have cousins,' he said, as if that it explained it all. Evie didn't say anything, but her look must have told him all he needed to know. 'Lots of female Italian cousins. They make it their business to ensure that my place is up to scratch.'

Evie nodded and Tom shrugged.

'Personally, I think they just like to spend my money.' Evie smiled then; it was a strange concept to her. Firstly, to have family like that; but also to be able to spend money on extras. Whilst she made a reasonable salary in her job, it barely covered the basics and Alice's university fees. She could feel Tom's eyes studying her. It wasn't an uncomfortable feeling, which surprised her as usually she avoided the scrutiny of others. Evie couldn't help but frown as she wondered why that was.

'Well, I'll leave you in peace. I'm right next door if you need anything.'

Evie nodded.

'You are safe here,' he added, as if he was concerned that her frown represented fear. Evie was happy to let him think that, since she needed some time to examine her own feelings. 'The apartment is alarmed and the entrance is guarded.'

Evie forced herself to focus on Tom and smiled.

'Thank you,' she said her voice feeling rusty as if it was something she hadn't said for many years. 'I appreciate all that you have done.' A small voice in her head wanted to add something about how glad she was he had decided to break some of the rules, but she thought better of it. They stood there for a moment, in the half-light from the kitchen, frozen in time. Neither of them said a word, but they seemed to reach an understanding, and they both turned away.

Evie stepped in to the guest room and closed the door behind her. As if she doubted her resolve in the moment, she stood with her back resting against it. She leaned her head back and closed her eyes, trying to figure out what was going on and to pinpoint an emotion in the swirl that was in her head, but her mind wouldn't let her. With a sigh, she walked over to the bed and stripped off her clothes, which by now were in desperate need of a wash — or possibly a dustbin. She pulled the fresh t-shirt over her head and smoothed it down to her knees. Unconsciously, she pulled at the neckline and sniffed. The sweet smell of flowers made her frown once more. Apparently, Tom's cousins did his washing too.

There was a mirror beside the door and she caught a glimpse of herself. What are you doing? she mouthed wordlessly. She gave herself a stern look and then said 'Alice,' out loud. It was enough to push the tumble of emotions from her brain and cause her to focus on the only important thing right now. Alice, she had to find Alice. There was nothing she could do at the moment. She had no idea where to start, and even if she wanted to, she suspected that leaving the apartment would set off the alarms that Tom had told her would keep her safe. No, all she could do now was clean up and get some sleep.

★ ★ ★

Evie turned over and tried to work out where she was. Her mind seemed to be trying to tell her something, but she couldn't work out the message in her sleep-addled state. She forced herself to pay attention. She was lying in a large bed and she was alone. There was a flash of something like disappointment at the thought, but she pushed it away with a frown. A small amount of light was seeping into the room under heavy curtains, and there was noise — a low mumble, but she couldn't make out what it was.

Slipping her feet out of bed, Evie made her away across the deep carpet, barefoot. Her mind had started to put the pieces together, and memories of yesterday flooded her. She was at Tom's place. He had rescued her once again, and then told her that the only way he could keep her safe was to keep her close to him. He had also mentioned breaking the rules, and she was sure this was one of the breaches. At the bedroom door, she leaned in, and could make out that the quiet mumble of voices, one a much lower pitch than the other. Evie wondered if the higher voice was one of the cousins that Tom had spoken of.

As quietly as she could, she pulled down on the handle and opened the door a fraction. The voices resolved into Tom's and a woman's. The woman was speaking English with no trace of an Italian accent. The words were indistinct, and Evie wondered if she should risk opening the door wider. Something told her that she should keep her presence secret, although whether that was to protect Tom from the consequences of his rule-breaking or to perhaps find out information he hadn't yet shared with her, Evie wasn't sure.

She pushed on the door but held tightly onto the handle with one hand, just to make sure it didn't fly from her grip, and risked a quick peep in the direction of the living area. Evie could see Tom — or, rather, the back of him. He was dressed in a dark suit, but she could see he hadn't put on his shoes yet. Evie wondered if the visitor had been expected.

'Where is she?' the voice asked. It was definitely feminine, and the tone was familiar. She could hear heels clicking on the wooden floors. A tall woman swept into view and then quickly out again, but it was enough for Evie to know who the other voice belonged to. Tom's boss, the Deputy Consul, Elizabeth Sullivan, was here.

11

Evie quickly wriggled back, suddenly worried that her hiding place would be discovered. Tom worked for Ms Sullivan and was presumable following her instructions, so why was he hiding the fact that she was secreted in his guest room?

'I have her somewhere safe.' Tom's voice was even, but Evie thought she could detect something in his tone, something he was fighting to keep hidden, and it made her mind race. Was he keeping her hidden for her own protection? Did she needed protecting from a senior official in the British Foreign Service, or was it for another reason?

Evie could feel her heart beating in her chest, and it sounded so loud to her ears that she moved softly away from the door, as if she was afraid that she would be heard. The problem was, she didn't know who to trust. Her gut told her Tom. He, at least, had acted to protect her and seemed invested in finding Alice, whereas Ms Sullivan seemed invested in not ruining her relationship with the local police, making politics more important than a missing woman. But Evie's previous experience told her that it was not always the obvious person who might betray you.

She felt a sudden flash of anger. Had she been taken in by Tom's manner and the way he appeared to care? She shook her head and clenched her fists. One thing she did know: no one was going to stand between her and Alice. Not the British government, not the local police, and certainly not Tom De Santis, however charming he might appear. What she needed was more information, preferably the unfiltered sort. If she wasn't sure if she could trust either of them, then it was unlikely that what they told her to her face would be the truth, so she needed to find out as much as she could when they thought she wasn't listening. With that she moved, as silently as she could, back to the door, so that she could once again listen to what she hoped would be an unguarded conversation.

'Have the *polizia* given you any further information?'

Tom's voice was rewarded with a snort. 'As usual, they are playing their cards close to their chest. Very unimaginatively. As is their custom, they underestimate us. There is clearly an international connection to this business, and so it's not something the British government is prepared to ignore.'

'And the life of a British citizen is at stake.'

There was silence, and Evie could only imagine the look on Ms Sullivan's face. She doubted that it would reflect any kind of concern.

'Naturally, if we can resolve that, it would make life easier for all involved.'

There was a pause, and Evie felt it was pointed, as if a silent conversation was occurring. 'But I don't need to remind you of your duty in this matter.'

'You are right, you don't need to remind me,' Tom said; his voice remained even, but Evie could feel the temperature drop.

'I have given you a long rein to achieve your aim. Don't let me down.'

'No, ma'am.'

Evie was frozen to the spot as she tried to process all that she had heard. Moving away from the door, she shuffled along the carpet until she could rest her head against the wall. She had heard a significant part of their conversation, but she wasn't sure that she knew what it meant. Her gut was telling her that Tom was on her side, but she couldn't be sure.

'Did you get all that?'

Evie jumped and put a hand to her chest as if she needed to be sure her heart was still there.

'What?' was about all she could think

to say in that moment. She looked up to see Tom De Santis looking down at her. He was leaning against the door frame and looked vaguely amused.

'Some of it,' Evie said as she struggled to find her feet.

He tipped his head to one side in a unspoken question.

'Why didn't you tell her I was here?' Evie asked. It was the first of her million questions that her mind could get a fix on.

She could feel Tom studying her, but she held his gaze and raised her chin defiantly. She wasn't going to look away until he told her what was going on. Tom seemed to come to a decision.

'Let's just say we don't always agree on priorities.'

'And what is that supposed to mean?' Evie demanded, her anger flaring. Tom took a step towards her and Evie moved back into the bedroom. What she didn't need right now was to be distracted by his nearness. Tom, for his part, nodded slightly and stood in the doorway.

'I want to find Alice.'

Evie swallowed. Hearing those words from someone else made the glimmer of hope flare inside her. She stared at his face looking for any signs of deceptions. He could, after all, just be telling her what she wanted to hear.

'And she doesn't?' Evie wasn't sure why she had asked, since she was sure she knew the answer.

'She does,' Tom said, choosing his words carefully. 'But she has other factors to consider.'

'More important than my sister?' Evie said incredulously.

'I know you don't want to hear this, Eve, but Alice is a small part of a much bigger picture.'

Evie turned away from him as she tried to marshal her emotions. She wouldn't let anything get in her way — not any bigger picture, and certainly not a political one.

'I don't care,' she said, turning on the spot to face him. He remained standing in the doorway as if he had received the message that she needed physical distance loud and clear.

'I don't expect you to, but you do need to understand what is at stake.'

Evie didn't trust herself to reply to this comment, so merely raised an eyebrow.

'Fraud is all about money,' he said, searching her face. Evie knew he was checking she was listening, so she nodded and shrugged. That much she knew.

'The questions which have to be asked are: Where is that money going? What is it for?'

Evie frowned and then shook her head, but Tom didn't elaborate.

'What is it for?' she said impatiently.

'We don't know for sure, but we have our suspicions.'

Again, he fell silent, and Evie had to resist the urge to cross the room and shake him to get him to speak.

'And what are your suspicions?' Evie forced the words through her clenched teeth.

'That, I can't tell you.'

'Because you don't know?'

'Because it is a matter of national security.'

Evie snorted. Seriously! He was now going to play the top-secret card? Tom's expression didn't change.

'Kidnapping a British citizen is not something that would be undertaken lightly, Eve. It's a very public act, likely to attract wide media attention. Either they had no choice or they simply don't care.'

Evie felt behind her for the edge of the bed and sat down. It didn't seem possible that the reality of the situation could be worse than what her imagination had been able to conjure up, but apparently it was.

'They're never going to let her go.' Her voice sounded hollow to her ears, and she knew it wasn't a question, more of a statement of fact.

'Not willingly, no,' Tom said. He moved towards her slowly as if she were a wild animal that might be easily startled. 'It is possible that she knows too much about the operation.'

Evie felt the breath catch in her throat, and the physical pain of loss was so sudden that she felt as if she had been punched in the stomach. She drew her knees up to her chest and buried her face. Alice was gone and she was never going to see her again. It was a thought that she had forced from her mind every time it had appeared since Alice had vanished, but now she was unable to push it away.

'Evie.' Tom's voice was soft but firm. 'Whilst Alice still has a purpose, whilst she is making them money, they will keep her safe. They won't hurt her.' The unspoken words hung in the air: *They won't hurt her if she does what they ask.*

Evie closed her eyes and sent a silent prayer to Alice, wherever she was. 'Just do what they say, Ally. Paint for them.'

When Evie opened her eyes, Tom was kneeling in front of her.

'What can we do?' Evie asked.

'We track under-the-table art sales. Anything off the books.'

Evie sniffed.

'But won't buyers know that they are fakes?' Evie just couldn't put all the pieces together.

Tom nodded. 'Yes, which is why there must be more to the plan. And that is what we are going to find out.'

Evie ran a hand over his face.

'We?' she asked, looking down at him. Tom gave a wry smile.

'It seems the only way to keep your size-six feet from trampling all over my investigation and out of their hands is to keep you close by.'

Evie couldn't help but smile. Finally she was going to be involved in finding her sister. She walked towards the door.

'Evie?'

'Yes?' she said without turning around.

'You're going to need to put some clothes on. You can't be inconspicuous in Rome wearing only an oversized t-shirt.'

12

Evie looked down, and only then remembered what she was wearing. She winced as the blush started to form on her cheeks. She didn't relish the thought of putting on the clothes she had previously slept in, but they would have to do. She padded barefoot across the hall into the bathroom. She had folded her clothes and left them there the night before, she was sure of it.

'Your clothes have gone to the laundry.' Tom's voice sounded further away, as if he were now in the kitchen area of the apartment. 'Have a look in the wardrobe. You should find something that will do.'

Evie frowned and walked back into the bedroom. She rolled back the fitted wardrobe door and found a row of outfits. She couldn't help but wonder who they belonged to. She had seen no evidence that Tom shared his apartment with anyone, and on closer inspection the outfits were a range of sizes. She pulled out a pair of beige linen trousers and a navy-blue chiffon top. Even to Evie's unfashionable eye they screamed expensive. Part of her wanted to find out where they came from, who they belonged to, but she shook her head and firmly told herself to get a grip. What difference did it make? She had no business prying into Tom's personal life; and besides, there were much more important things at stake. An image of Alice, alone and afraid, swam into her mind and she shuddered. It was enough to get her back across the room and into the shower. They had work to do.

In the kitchen, Tom had laid out a full continental breakfast. The pastries smelled as if they had come straight from a bakery, which Evie suspected they had.

'Don't we have things we need to be doing?' she asked impatiently, but her stomach gave her away. A hollow growl seemed to echo around the walls, and she self-consciously put her hand to her belly that had betrayed her.

'We do, but first we eat,' Tom said. Again, the shadow of a smile pulled at his lips.

Evie opened her mouth to argue, but one look from Tom told her she was wasting her time so instead she slipped onto one of the tall bar stools and took a sip of the coffee that was waiting for her. She almost let out a murmur of appreciation at the rich brew, but managed to catch herself in time.

'Can we at least talk about the plan?'

'If you can eat and listen at the same time?'

Evie frowned at the tone. She had hoped they would be partners in this mission, but Tom sounded like her grandad whenever she spent money on something he considered frivolous — usually something for Alice. Not trusting herself to speak, knowing that a complaint about his tone might trigger a lengthy discussion, Evie merely nodded and helped herself to a croissant dusted with almonds.

'We have two lines of enquiry. If they are creating fakes, then they must have a way to shift them to buyers.'

Tom took a sip of his coffee and Evie nodded again.

'But, as you rightly pointed out, no buyer is going to spend good money on a fake.'

Evie raised an eyebrow, and Tom held up his hands as if he was conceding the point. 'However good it might be. So there must be a plan to deal with that problem.'

Evie took a moment to think.

'Replace the real art with the fakes?' she said, as if she were thinking out loud. 'If the plan was just to steal the real art, then there would be no point producing a copy.' In her head, Evie added: *or taking Alice.* As Tom said nothing, Evie looked up, wondering if she had suggested something foolish, but his face only registered that he was impressed. Evie pushed down the warm feeling that bloomed in her chest; she didn't have time to go all googly-eyed over this man.

'My thoughts exactly,' Tom said

'So, that's what we need to find out. How are we going to do it?' That part, Evie had no clue about, and she sincerely hoped that Tom did.

'Let's just say, I know a guy,' he said with a grin.

Evie slipped from her bar stool and grabbed the pair of sunglasses that she had found in a drawer in the guest room.

'Well?' she asked. 'What are we waiting for?'

For a split second, Evie wondered if Tom had changed his mind — if he had decided that she needed to stay here in the apartment, where she might conceivably be safe. However safe it might be, it was the last place she wanted to be, and so she started to form an argument in her mind — the primary point being, there was no way she was just going to stay behind, so he might as well just take her with him — but there was no need. If that had been an idea in Tom's mind, it was quickly gone.

'How's your acting?' he said.

Evie blinked; that was just about the last thing she expected him to say. She shrugged.

'The person I'm going to see thinks I'm a British businessman. He doesn't know of my connection to the Embassy.'

Evie nodded, but didn't understand the point.

'So, you can't be Eve Spencer who is looking for her sister.' He said the words slowly as if she might have difficulty understanding, and without conscious thought Eve rolled her eyes. Tom studied her for a moment, and Evie knew what was coming next. She was going to have to pretend to be his girlfriend.

'You'll need to be my sister Caroline.'

Evie wasn't sure whether to be relieved or insulted. Did he think she couldn't pull off being his girlfriend? Or maybe this mystery person had actually met Tom's girlfriend. Perhaps that explained the clothes hanging in the wardrobe?

'Sure,' she said, as nonchalantly as possible. Evie thought she saw something flash in Tom's eyes, and she wondered if he had guessed at her thoughts. She turned away to look for the shoes she had kicked off the night before. Whilst the shoes in the wardrobe were amazing, none of them were her size, so her deck shoes would just have to do. Evie worked hard at composing her face to hide any remains of emotion.

'Anything I need to know? About being your sister?' Evie tried to keep her voice casual, but she wasn't sure she had succeeded.

'Caroline calls me 'Tommo', but apart from that, no. Piero hasn't actually met my sister.'

'Tommo.' Evie tried out the word, but it sounded strange on her lips; it didn't seem to fit the man standing in front of her, who seemed far too sophisticated and in control to be called such a name.

'That's me. Just play your part and

don't ask too many questions.'

Evie raised an eyebrow.

'You mean, not trampling your investigation with my size-six shoes?'

Tom didn't look fazed by her retort.

'Exactly,' he said, before picking up his grey suit jacket and pulling it on. 'Just follow my lead.' He grabbed his keys and moved towards the door. 'If I ask what time we are meeting Francesca, then that means we need to get out of there as soon as possible.'

Evie stared at his back as he walked away from her. She couldn't quite believe that her life had gone from working long hours in a boring job to this. Life and the movies had seemed poles apart, but now — now it just felt like she had unwittingly accepted a part in a blockbuster spy movie.

'Secret code word?' she said, but more to herself than to Tom. He held the door open for her.

'Prepare for the worst-case scenario.'

Evie felt a shiver of fear but she ignored it. If she was afraid going to meet a man who might have some information that could help them, with Tom by her side, then how was Alice feeling right now? The thought gave her the strength she needed to follow Tom out of the door.

They walked through the concierge hall of the apartment block and Tom nodded to the man in uniform. He quickly stepped around his desk and held the main doors open for them. At the kerb was a sleek black limo, and the driver stood ready with the door open. Evie was glad she was wearing sunglasses to disguise her surprise and did her best to slide elegantly into the back seat. She started to shift across to make room for Tom, but the door was closed firmly behind her. Evie felt panic start to swell. Was this another trap? But before her mind could race too far down that road, the door on her other side was opened by the driver and Tom stepped in, unbuttoning his jacket as he did so. Evie tried to appear as if she had not just had a mini panic attack, but it was clear that Tom had picked up on it.

'Relax, Eve. We're just going to see an old acquaintance.'

Evie frowned and gestured her head towards the driver. She had expected to be 'Caroline' from now on.

'One of ours,' Tom said simply. His hand moved across the space between them, and Evie felt him briefly squeeze her hand. When she looked up, Tom's gaze was focused firmly on the buildings passing quickly by as the limo driver wove his way through the busy streets.

13

Evie tried to keep track of the route they had taken, but she was soon lost. The driver seemed to know the city well, and was taking side routes and small alleys to reach their destination. The car finally stopped, and the driver climbed quickly out and opened the door for Evie, who slipped her feet out onto the pavement and accepted the hand that was offered to assist her. Tom spoke to the driver and then held out his arm for Evie, who, getting into role, crooked her arm through his, and they walked together across the pavement to a large glass-fronted building.

Two security men in uniform, with guns strapped to their belts, unlocked the doors and held them open so that Tom and Evie could walk through. Evie felt a slight increased pressure on her arm; she knew Tom was telling her this was normal and she shouldn't be concerned. Once inside, Evie was surprised at how light and airy the building felt. Looking up, she could see natural light pouring through the glass roof, and so she lifted a hand to remove her sunglasses. It was a white open space with artwork and sculptures hanging from invisible hooks and wires that gave the impression everything was floating in mid-air. Evie had no idea if Caroline would have been impressed by this kind of thing, but she couldn't help but let a little of that show. Alice, she thought, would love this.

A tall, thin woman dressed head to toe in black appeared.

'Signor Piero will be with you shortly.' The woman's English was perfect save for the Italian accent. 'He begs your forgiveness for the delay and asks that you use the time to admire his new additions.' The woman held out her right hand and nodded, before disappearing once again.

Evie allowed herself to be pulled

towards a large painting that appeared, to her eye, to have been drawn by a toddler and then blown up to the size of her kitchen wall at home. It was modern art, something that Evie couldn't quite get her head around.

'Bold use of colours,' Tom said, but Evie wasn't sure if he genuinely thought that and was simply concerned their conversation was being monitored.

'It certainly has a deconstructed quality to it.'

Tom turned briefly to her with a look of surprise. Evie smiled; she could fake art appreciation with the best of them. She had spent many a Sunday afternoon in the free modern art galleries in London — 'practising pretension', as Alice had called it. Alice was definitely a traditionalist when it came to the art she loved. Evie leaned in, unable to resist the urge to comment further.

'I particularly like the finger-painting aspect. Reminds me of my early work at pre-school.'

Tom's eyes flashed dangerously, but

he was struggling to wipe the amusement from his face and she got the distinct feeling that he agreed with her assessment.

'Signor De Santis, a thousand pardons.' A short, petite man appeared, dressed in a three-piece suit that would not have looked out of place a hundred years ago.

'And this must be the lovely Caroline.' He held out his hand and Evie returned the gesture before finding her hand lifted to his lips and kissed. Evie forced herself to smile and not act like she wanted to yank her hand away.

'It's a pleasure to finally meet you,' she said with a nod of her head. 'Tommo has told me so much about you.'

'In that case, don't believe a word he says,' Piero said, dropping the heavily accented Italian for a voice that would not have been out of place near where Evie lived back in England.

Evie fought to hide the surprise she felt.

'Relax, sweetheart. Me being a Londoner is the worst-kept secret in Rome, but the punters seem to like it, even expect it; so in public I'm Signor Piero. In private, my friends call me Pete.'

Pete turned his attention back to Tom.

'So, Tommo, why have you brought your lovely sister here to see me today?'

Tom shrugged.

'Caroline's over from London for a visit. I'm taking her out to lunch, but we have some business to discuss first?'

Pete looked between Evie and Tom, and Evie kept her face neutral as if she had no idea what that business might be.

'In that case, perhaps the lovely Caroline can have a look round and we can discuss matters out the back?'

Evie watched as Tom strode off towards the back of the gallery. This had not been part of her plan, to be left out of an important meeting, but she knew that making a fuss now would not

128

help their cause, and so she decided she had to play her part. She would discuss this development with Tom later. She moved around the gallery, studying each piece of work in turn. The prices for some pieces were eye-watering, and for others she could only assume they were so ridiculously high that the proprietor was embarrassed to actually write the numbers down — either that, or they had too many zeros to fit on the small white cards.

She kept her movements casual, and made sure to spend what she considered to be an appropriate length of time staring at each art form, but all the while she was ensuring that she was getting closer to the rear of the gallery and nearer to the door that Tom had disappeared through. A tiny collection of miniatures caught her eye. They were presented in heavy gilt frames, disproportionate to their size, and displayed one above the other. They were painted in traditional oils and muted tones, and so managed to stand out from their more garish companions. Evie walked towards them and studied each in turn.

'Signorina De Santis has a fine eye.'

Evie jumped as she felt the presence beside her, not realising that the tall, willowy gallery employee had appeared beside her.

'They seem a little traditional for the gallery's clientele,' Evie answered, figuring it was something that Caroline might say.

'I found them both intriguingly traditional, yet modern. See the use of the tiny dots in the left-hand corner of each, almost as if it were a signature.'

Evie peered closer. She hadn't noticed before, but now they seemed to jump out at her: so small that she almost needed to press her nose against the canvas to see them, there were tiny pale pink dots, which somehow both blended in and stood out.

'A new artist?' Evie asked

'Yes, Signorina De Santis, Slovakian, I believe. Signor Piero could tell you more. That is, if you are interested?'

The question was asked in the way the shop assistants in exclusive clothes boutiques ask, a veiled question suggesting that perhaps you could not afford to purchase a carrier bag, let alone an item of clothing. Not that Evie chose to frequent them, but on occasion Alice had dragged her into them and she felt the same irritation at the superior manner.

'Hmm. I may ask my brother for a little pre-lunch treat, since he has made me wait so long.'

The other woman looked suitably chastised and went to move away.

'Of course, Signorina De Santis. Perhaps I can find out how long your brother will be?'

'That would be very kind,' Evie replied, doing her best impression of a rich and entitled woman. Despite everything, it was quite enjoyable playing this role, even for a short while. She couldn't imagine it, of course, not having to think about every penny that was spent. It was true that she was earning reasonable money now, but that had not always been the case, and Evie had not lost the habits that she had learnt during the lean times.

A few minutes, later the door opened and Tom reappeared.

'See anything you like?' he called as he walked towards her. Evie turned to him with her best pout.

'Well, since you made me wait so long out here by myself; yes, actually.' She walked towards the tiny miniatures and Tom followed her.

'I think that I deserve these since I've waited so long for you.' Just like she had before, Tom leaned in closer so that he could make out the paintings. Evie watched as his eyeline lowered and he took in the price tag.

'Actually, sis, I think we might be out of time.' He looked down at his wrist and held it up so that she could see his watch. 'What time are we meeting Francesca?'

The words seemed to echo around Evie's mind. She had just been messing with him, but now he had uttered those words. She swallowed the lump that had appeared in her throat and tried to remember what time it was, even though she had glanced at her own watch not two seconds ago.

'We're late,' she finally managed to say out loud. 'You shouldn't have taken so long.' She made herself look as if she were sulking. 'Now there is no time to buy me the gift you promised!' Tom's face played his part, managing to look apologetic and pacifying all at the same time.

'You are quite right, of course. I will make it up to you. How about a trip to Valentino's after lunch?'

Evie had no idea who or what Valentino's was, but she tried to look grudgingly pleased; and when Tom offered her his arm, she took it, and they strolled from the gallery as if they had no cares in the world.

Tom waited on the pavement until Evie had slid into the back seat, and then made his way around the car, waving off the driver and opening his door for himself. He said something to the driver, who moved the car quickly into the flow of traffic. Evie couldn't resist a glance behind them, but could not make out any sign that someone was following them, and only then did she allow herself to relax a little.

'Are we safe now?' she asked when it seemed that Tom was going to say anything.

'Of course,' he said, frowning slightly. 'You were never in any danger.'

Evie stared at him. 'So why did you use the code word?'

'Did you see the price of those miniatures? I'm on a government salary and have moderate business interests, Eve. I can't afford those kinds of prices.'

He said it as if he were discussing the weather, and so Evie glared at him in disbelief.

'I thought there was something wrong,' she managed to say between her clenched teeth.

'There was,' Tom said, as if it were the most obvious thing in the world. 'I thought I was going to have to sell my apartment just to keep up the ruse.'

14

Evie kept her eyes on the scenes passing by outside as she didn't trust herself to respond to Tom in that moment. Her anger cooled a little as she watched the people of Rome go about their business, but she wasn't about to let him off that easily.

'Did you find out anything useful?' She knew her voice was dripping with ice, but felt it was no less than he deserved.

'Pete's not involved.' Tom's reply was mild, as if her tone had been completely lost on him. Evie could feel the anger flare again. This was not a game. There was too much at stake — Alice's life, for starters.

'So it was a waste of time.' She made a statement rather than asked a question. She sensed that Tom was shaking his head, but she didn't turn around. A thought, a worrying thought, was starting to grow in her mind.

'Was that part of the plan, or just for my benefit?' She turned her face towards him as she said the words so that she could read any immediate reaction. Tom, for his part, kept his gaze steady, and Evie couldn't tell if the reaction was genuine or something he had been trained for.

'What benefit are you thinking?' Tom asked. 'An opportunity to look at some fine and extremely expensive artwork?'

Evie knew that he was toying with her. She felt the anger inside her turn white-hot but she refused to let any of it show.

'You know exactly what I mean.' She stared at him and let the words hang in the air for a moment. 'Is this just play-acting? To keep me away from the real task of finding my sister?' There, she had said the words out loud. His expression told her that he was weighing her up, so she forced all the emotion she felt down deep — something she was prac-tised at — and returned his gaze.

'Would you believe me if I said no?'

Now it was Tom's turn to assess to Evie's reaction. She took a moment to consider his question. 'Look me in the eye and tell me what just happened.'

She watched as he nodded his head slightly, then shifted in his seat so that he was twisted towards her.

'Eve. What you have just experienced was what we like to call a fishing trip.'

Tom paused, so Evie nodded to indicate that she was following him.

'Sometimes when you fish you catch the big one; other times you are left with small fry.'

Evie rolled her eyes now; she couldn't help it. 'Stop talking in riddles and tell me what happened.'

'Pete is a source, Evie. He exists on the fringes of criminality — mostly on the right side of the law, but occasionally he drifts. I have just tested the waters.'

Evie raised her eyebrows at yet another fishing-related expression, and Tom held his hands out in surrender, although she suspected he intended to veer back into the territory.

'Sorry. I wanted to see what, if anything, Pete had heard. He's a good person to go to for rumours and intel.'

Evie nodded but Tom said nothing and she could feel the frustration build again.

'So, what did he have to say? Or was that *top-secret*?' Evie mimed inverted commas with her fingers. She knew she was probably being unfair, but right now she didn't have the time or energy to do anything other than ask direct questions, even if she was coming across as rude.

'Not much,' Tom said. 'I couldn't come right out and ask him if he knew of any plans to swap masterpieces for fakes.' He glanced at Evie. 'Albeit good-quality fakes.' Despite her best efforts, Evie couldn't resist a smile, knowing that Tom was trying not to upset her.

'So it wasn't a waste of time?' she asked, but this time it was a question and not a dig.

'Sometimes it's about taking small

bits of information to form a bigger picture, and sometimes it's about the information people don't have.'

Evie frowned in confusion. It made no real sense to her.

'Something he hasn't told you?'

'More like something he doesn't know.'

Evie shrugged her shoulders and raised her eyebrows.

'Pete didn't have much to tell me, and so that raises two possibilities. Either he doesn't want to tell me something, or he doesn't know anything.'

'Okay . . . ' Evie said, still not seeing how that all joined up.

'Both tell us something. If he doesn't want to tell me something, then it is likely to involve some serious players who pose a threat; or whatever it is is above his pay grade, so to speak.'

Evie nodded. Now, that made more sense, though she would never have considered it like that.

'We have two lines of enquiry to

pursue. One: the possibility that Pete is afraid of whoever it is, and has been threatened to keep his mouth shut.'

Evie nodded, although that thought was not a comforting one. If someone was threatening Pete, then Alice was in serious trouble.

'Or, two: that whoever is behind this is removed from the national art scene and the slightly unlawful edges. Which could mean that this person is dealing with a private collector who has no intention of publicly displaying his art.'

'Does that help?' Evie wondered, before realising that she had said it out loud. She hadn't intended to, worried that it would sound like another criticism.

'It narrows the field from the whole world to two specific groups.' Tom turned his attention back to her, and Evie felt him reach out for her hand which was nearest to him. He gave it a brief squeeze.

'It's a step in the right direction. I know this is frustrating and scary, but we need to approach this whole thing logically. It is our best chance to find Alice.' He sounded like he wanted or needed her to believe him. For a moment, Evie allowed her doubts to cloud her mind before she pushed them away. She had not managed to get any closer to finding Alice by herself — maybe it was time to step outside her comfort zone and trust someone else. It frightened her, but the thought of losing Alice was so much worse that she knew she was prepared to take the risk.

'I know,' she said softly before adding, 'I trust you.' The words seemed so unfamiliar to Evie that she frowned as her mouth formed them. A quick glance at Tom registered surprise, and something else; but, as usual, it was quickly gone and replaced by his neutral expression.

'Good.' He looked like he was going to comment on her last statement, but seemed to think better of it. The silence seemed to build up between them, and it got to the point that Evie felt the urge to break it.

'So, what next?'

'Shopping,' Tom replied.

Evie stared. That wasn't exactly what she'd been expecting him to say. He gave her a small smile.

'You can't go to our next destination dressed like that.'

Evie looked down at herself. The clothes were not her own, but in truth they were of better quality than even her best outfit back home. Tom laughed.

'There's nothing wrong with you. It's just that our next stop has a dress code.'

Evie frowned.

'Don't worry. I know just the place and just the person to help us.'

The driver had taken them back into the heart of Rome's fashion district. The car slid to a stop outside one of the many boutiques, and the driver repeated his early action of holding the door for Evie as she climbed out, feeling — as before — out of place and inelegant. She looked up at the clothes displayed in the shop and started to shake her head. No way. There was no way she was going to walk into this exclusive shop and experience the fashion shame that comes when you are obviously out of your depth. Tom seemed oblivious and strode towards the door.

Evie heard the car engine come to life and watched in dismay as her possible exit route disappeared into the flow of traffic with a herald of honking horns. With no other choice, she scrambled after Tom, who was walking through the large glass doors which were being held open by a burly security guard in a high-end suit. Evie was sure the guard was staring at her, or maybe judging her, but he made no comment as she entered the inner sanctum. She tried to hold her head up high as she braced herself for the inevitable judgement which, even in Italian was going to be hard to hear.

Instead, she found herself grabbed — or, at least, that was what she thought was happening, when in fact she was being pulled into a tight hug.

'Tommo, he has told me all about you!' a heavily accented voice said into her ear. Evie found herself held at arm's length so that the beautiful shop assistant could see her face. 'He has told me all about you!'

All Evie could do was blink in surprise and wonder if this was Tom's girlfriend.

'I am Valentina; *famiglia*,' Valentina added with a twinkle in her eye, and Evie knew that she was going to lose her battle with the blush that was rising in her cheeks. She felt as if Valentina had read her mind when she'd reassured Evie that she was in fact family, and not a girlfriend past or present.

'Tommo, he is right. You are *bellissimo*.'

Even Evie knew enough Italian to understand the meaning of the word, and she looked at Tom, trying to hide her feelings from showing on her face. Tom seemed to be locked in a wordless battle with Valentina, who Evie supposed was one of his cousins. Evie looked away, feeling like she might be spying on a private moment, but also to give herself a chance to process the words that Tom had used to describe her. His reaction told her that Valentina was not making the comment up, and Evie wasn't sure how she felt about it. Her mind had wandered the night before, and she had considered all sorts of possibilities with Tom; but right now she needed to focus, and the idea that Tom might have similar feelings was a distraction that she couldn't afford.

15

The silent conversation was followed by rapid Italian that Evie couldn't follow. It involved a lot of arm-waving on Valentina's part; but whether this was because she was angry about something, or merely Italian, Evie couldn't tell. Tom remained stoically English throughout and so gave nothing away. Evie's eyes drifted to the stunning gowns of every style and length. Her eyes almost popped out of her head when she saw the associated price tags. There was no way she could afford any of this, not even a pair of stockings. She opened her mouth to speak, but in her gawping hadn't realised that Tom and Valentina's attention was now focused on her.

'Relax, Evie. We are borrowing, not buying.'

Evie relaxed a little at the thought

that she wasn't about to max out her credit cards when she realised there was another pressing concern. Tom expected her to wear one of these amazing gowns to a place where the dress code required it. To say that was out of Evie's comfort zone was an understatement: she still struggled to order a drink at a busy pub, and that was about the extent of her social life back home. She had never been to a black tie event, had no idea of the etiquette involved, and this did not seem the time for her to try and learn on the job.

'I can't . . . ' she said, but Valentina held up her hands and started to fire off rapid Italian.

'Valentina is a master. She will find you something both comfortable and stunning,' Tom translated. Evie felt the embarrassment well up again at the fact that her face was clearly so readable. She didn't have any time to comment further, as Valentina had grabbed her hand and was dragging her off to the changing rooms at the back of the store.

Two hours later, and they were back at Tom's apartment, loaded with shopping bags. Evie suspected that the normal reaction to the type of event they were going to attend was excitement and expectation, but she couldn't summon up any of those feelings. There was too much at stake, and she couldn't shake the sense that she was going to somehow let Alice down through her lack of social graces. The high-end designer bags sat on the kitchen work surface, and Evie felt as if they were taunting her.

'Relax, Eve. All you need to do is smile and listen to conversation.'

Evie wasn't sure whether this comment was encouraging or insulting. She had never been asked to be 'arm candy' before, and she wasn't about to start now. Her mind tried to form a response that wouldn't come out as plain rude when Tom laughed softly. Evie turned to him.

'I'm not suggesting that you are only there to look pretty, but the reality is that rich men will show off in front of a beautiful woman, and we may find that you learn more from this evening than I do.'

How was it that this man could read her so easily? It was unsettling, and something she wasn't used to. She also wasn't sure if she liked it or not. To distract herself from his words, which had made her heart go jittery, she focused on saying something, anything that would be a suitable 'no comment'-type response.

'I think you have way too much faith in my ability to speak Italian.'

Evie could have sworn that Tom's eyes were sparkling in amusement.

'That won't be necessary. Since the host of the evening is the UK Ambassador to Italy, the guests will speak English, out of respect for his position.'

If Evie had been concerned before, now she was both confused and terrified.

'We are going to a party hosted by

the UK Ambassador to find out information about Alice?' She needed a moment to process this information. Her mind was racing, and so she stood up from her seat and walked towards the windows that looked over the street below. If the people involved in Alice's kidnapping were friendly with the highest UK government representative in the land, then could she trust anyone? Could she trust Tom, even? The familiar feelings of suspicion and the need to tackle this problem alone threatened to overwhelm her. She pulled her arms in tight around her middle, something that she had been doing since she was a child and which was strangely comforting. The hand on her arm made her jump, even though she knew the only person it could be was Tom.

'What about Ms Sullivan? Even dressed up, she is bound to recognise me.'

'She won't be there,' Tom answered reassuringly. 'A senior member of the team always stays away to deal with any issues, and to ensure if something were to happen at the event, we would still have a senior operative in Rome.'

Evie stared: this was not a comforting thought.

'Relax; there will be a lot of rich and famous people there tonight, but I don't believe that any of them are directly involved.'

Evie forced herself to turn and face him, needing to see his expression. It was one of confidence and reassurance, but Evie could still feel the small spark of distrust.

'The market for hot pieces of art is limited, due to the sheer cost and risk of the purchase. There will be many intermediaries involved, and it is likely that the ultimate buyer will have no idea of the circumstances of it becoming available.'

Now it was Evie's turn to look incredulous. How could they not know? She voiced this to Tom, and her words came out stronger than she intended. He responded by holding his hands up in mock surrender.

'Perhaps I should have said that they choose to remain oblivious of the process.'

'Too rich to care?' Evie retorted with a steely expression, her eyes drifting to the artwork and ceramics that filled his apartment.

'Unfortunately, yes,' Tom said, his face serious. 'I'm not condoning the behaviour, but it may work in our favour. We may hear some information that points us to an intermediary, who could in turn lead us to Alice.'

Evie took a moment to digest this point of view. She didn't have to like or approve of these people, but if they were a means to an end then she would put on a good show. It was just acting a part, after all. She nodded slowly, her eyes drifting to the art deco clock on the wall.

'What time do I need to be ready?'

Tom glanced at his watch.

'Valentina will be here in about half an hour.'

'Valentina's coming?' Evie asked,

thinking it might be easier if she had someone with her who she could copy in all things etiquette.

'No, but she insisted on helping you get ready.' Tom shrugged as if to imply that it was an Italian thing. Once again, Evie wasn't sure if this was going to be good or bad, but one thing was certain: Valentina would make sure that, at the very least, she looked the part.

Evie had never spent so much time getting ready. Valentina had arrived, directed her to the shower, and loaded her down with beauty products. It had taken over an hour to dry and style her hair, which was now carefully coiled in a smooth and shiny chignon. Her makeup had taken a further hour, and when Evie was finally permitted to look in the mirror, she barely recognised herself. A little of the tension left her shoulders when she realised that she would look as if she belonged at the party, even if she felt like a fish out of water.

Valentina helped her into her silk

gown which was emerald green and fitted her curves in all the right places. She had never felt so on display in her life, but a quick peek in the mirror told her it would have the effect on men that they were looking for. Valentina turned her around so that she was facing the mirror.

'*Bellissimo*,' Valentina said softly with a small smile. 'I think all eyes will be on you tonight.' And she squeezed Evie's shoulders. Despite all her misgivings, Evie couldn't help but feel a little like Cinderella after she had been made over by her fairy godmother. Evie had never really understood the whole 'getting dolled up' thing, but she had to admit that it was a nice feeling.

'And now we will show Tommo. Check he approves, yes?'

Evie's heart did the jittery thing again. She gave herself a little shake. It was just nerves about the evening ahead; it wasn't as if Tom cared what she looked like, as long as she could pass for whatever character he needed her to be. Valentina reached the door and held out a hand, which Evie took, trying to remember all of her new friend's tips about walking elegantly in heels.

When they reached the main living area, Tom was standing looking out of the window onto the moonlit streets below. He was dressed all in black, and his suit showed off his fit and lean body. At the sound of her heels clicking on the wooden floor, he turned and opened his mouth to speak. Whatever he was going to say died on his lips, and instead he simply stared. For a moment, Tom and Evie were frozen in a tableau, until an amused cough from Valentina broke the spell.

'Evie, you look . . . perfect,' he said, seemingly remembering who he was and what lay ahead of them that evening. Evie watched him switch back to professional mode as he crossed the space between them and held up the shrug that Valentina had also borrowed from work. He slipped it carefully around Evie's shoulders and then held out an arm, which she accepted, telling herself it was because she was worried about taking a wrong step in her two-inch heels.

'Who am I supposed to be tonight?' she asked as they settled in to the back seat of the chauffer-driven car.

'My sister Caroline again,' he replied.

'So, you are going as you?' she asked.

Tom rewarded her with a laugh. 'I'm always me.'

'Yes,' she said, rolling her eyes. 'But are you Tom De Santis the businessman, or Tom De Santis the British government agent?'

'Tonight, Evie, I am personal security for the Ambassador.'

Evie's face fell. She had an awful feeling that she was going to be abandoned the moment they arrived.

'Due to my seniority, I get to attend the party as a guest, but my primary role is to guard the Ambassador and his family. The Ambassador will introduce me as Tom the businessman.'

Evie stared at him.

'Your life is complicated.'

'You're telling me,' he said, before his face broke into a grin, 'But it keeps it interesting.'

16

Their car joined a winding queue of other expensive vehicles waiting to pass through security at the gates to the Ambassador's residence. From the side window Evie could see handsome men of all ages assisting glamorous women step from their chariots. She whispered a little prayer of thanks for Valentina's close attention to detail in an area where Evie was basically clueless. Though she was usually impatient with queues, this one moved too fast for Evie, and soon it was their turn.

Tom got out of the car first, buttoned his tuxedo jacket, and walked around to open her door. He held out his hand to her as he gave a subtle nod to the security on the door. The two men in suits barely gave any acknowledgment, so it was clear to Evie that everyone else would consider them simply guests that evening.

As she found her feet — not easy after a combination of trying to elegantly exit a car with a long and tight gown on, and then stand on heels — she felt Tom lean in to her.

'Relax, and maybe try to smile.'

With a jolt, Evie realised that her expression was probably not one of a person about to attend a glamorous soirée. She tried to smile.

'Better,' he whispered. 'But remember you are going to a party, not an execution.'

Evie jabbed Tom in the ribs with her elbow as she turned to smile at a couple who were walking up the red carpet to the double-front doors, which led into a high-ceilinged entrance hall, completed with a wide wooden spiral staircase.

They followed the line of guests, who were passing pleasantries with a man who Evie knew could only be the host, and a younger woman who she assumed was his wife.

'Mr De Santis. A pleasure to see you, as always.'

Evie watched as they shook hands like a host and a guest, not an employer and employee.

'Mr Ambassador, may I introduce my sister, Caroline De Santis, who is visiting from England this week.'

The Ambassador turned his practiced gracious smile in Evie's direction and reached for her hand to shake. Not knowing whether it was protocol or not, Evie shook it, and then found herself kissed on both cheeks.

'A pleasure to meet you, Ms De Santis. I hope you are enjoying all that Italy has to offer.'

Evie smiled, and tried not to let the fact that nothing could be much farther from the truth on that score show on her face.

'Rome is a beautiful city, but I have to confess I have come here for the artwork.'

Out of the corner of her eye Evie thought she saw Tom's smile go tight just for a second, and she filed away that reaction in her head to consider later.

'In that case, I hope Tom is finding the time to take you to all our art galleries. There are many to choose from.'

Evie nodded and smiled before greeting the Ambassador's wife and finding herself moving with the flow of people to a much larger room which had been set out for the occasion. Tom manoeuvred them to a clear spot and helped himself to two glasses of champagne from a passing waiter. He handed one to Evie, who raised a questioning eyebrow, thinking that drinking on the job might not be the best thing.

'Just for show,' he said softly, so that only she could hear.

She smiled and took the smallest sip before turning towards him.

'Does the Ambassador know who I really am?' she asked.

Tom didn't respond, just raised an eyebrow, which Evie took as a definite no. Evie didn't quite know what to do with this new information. It seemed like every step they took raised the stakes even higher.

'Why don't you mingle? I need to attend to something. I will only be a moment.' Tom flashed her a smile and was gone before she could offer any argument. This, she thought to herself, was exactly the type of situation she'd been worried about. She had no idea how to mingle. Did you just walk up to people and hang around close by until they turned to talk to you? Even the thought of that made her wince. She scanned the room looking for someone in a similar situation — perhaps she could find an ally somewhere. Then an image of Alice swam into her mind and she knew what she had to do. She was here to gather any snippets of information that might help her find her sister, and no amount of fear or uncertainty was going to stop her from doing just that.

Eve's eyes fell on a man in a white tuxedo, and his partner, who was of a similar age and knew how to dress. They appeared to be the flame for the party's moths, and so they seemed a good a place to start as any. She took one step forward, her eyes focused firmly on her goal, and then her view was blocked. Evie looked up to find a young man in a somewhat ill-fitting black tuxedo standing closer than etiquette seemed to allow.

'Eve Spencer?' he asked softly, his English perfect but his accent giving away the fact that he was Italian born and bred.

Evie blinked. At no point had Tom told her what to do if someone recognised her. The chances of that had seemed highly unlikely . . . unless this handsome young man had something to do with Alice's captors. She scanned the room but there was no sign of Tom. She could make a scene, of course, although she didn't feel any menace from the man — but what if he had something to tell her? In that split second, Evie made up her mind. She smiled and indicated with her head that he should follow her to one of the outer rooms where there were fewer guests. A risk, she knew, but she couldn't have this conversation out in the open.

They stepped in to another equally beautiful room, and as they passed through the doors the background noise dropped to a low hum of murmured conversation. Finding a spot near to the patio doors which showed an exquisitely maintained courtyard beyond, Evie turned to her companion.

'Yes?' she asked, deciding that she would say as little as possible. The young man seemed relieved, but mostly his face portrayed fear and fatigue. A look that Evie could relate to. She frowned, wondering if this man had been forced to come here under duress.

'My name is Roberto Bianchi.'

Evie nodded, not wanting to break the spell. She was certain now that this man had something important to tell her.

'I am a friend of Alice.'

Evie's heart contracted, wondering if that were true or just part of the grand game she seemed to be playing.

'A very close friend.' He seemed to stumble over the words.

'I have been away.' His words started to come out faster and in a tumble, his accent getting thicker as he spoke. 'I work for the gallery. I am very junior but I am learning restoration and evaluation. I was sent to a rural gallery to appraise a painting.' He waved his hands as if to tell himself that these details did not matter. 'I had not heard from Alice. I was worried, of course, but I know her.' He smiled to himself. 'Sometimes she gets lost in her work. I need to remind her to eat.'

Evie relaxed a little. His description of Alice fitted her own almost perfectly, and so her gut told her this young man was genuinely a friend of her sister — and, most likely, something more.

'When I return, I visit her home, the school, even the galleries, but I can find no trace. Everyone tells me she has gone. *Gone where?* I ask. But nobody knows.'

Roberto looked at Evie, and she saw her own grief and fear reflected in his face.

'They tell me she is an artist and is following her art. But I know Alice. My Alice would not leave without a word . . . And then I find out you are here. Her beloved sister, who she talks about often and I know. She would not leave without sending word to you, not my Alice.'

Roberto seemed to run out of breath, and Evie reached out a hand to rest on his arm.

'You are right; she wouldn't,' Evie replied softly.

'Then where is she?' Roberto started to pace and run a hand through his hair, leaving it slightly ruffled.

'I don't know,' Evie said, and saw what little colour there was left on Roberto's face blanch. 'But I will find her.'

Roberto stopped pacing.

'Someone has taken her. Yes?'

Evie flashed him a warning look and

Roberto walked past her, tried one of the patio doors, and stepped outside into the courtyard. Evie searched once more for any sign of Tom, but finding her gaze empty, followed Roberto outside.

'I told her to be careful,' Roberto said softly, obviously picking up on the need to be discreet in discussing such matters. Evie could hear running water, and her eyes drifted to the central fountain that was carefully decorated with soft white fairy lights.

'Careful of what?' Evie asked, trying to rein in her excitement at new information that might provide another piece of the puzzle.

'Careful of who saw her paint.' Roberto turned away. 'The postcards she painted for you . . . Her ability to mimic other styles is impressive — beautiful, even — but also dangerous.'

17

Evie started a little as Roberto uttered those words. Had he really worked this out by himself, or was he somehow involved?

'But who saw her paint?' Evie asked, deciding that whatever Roberto's involvement, he might be able to provide her with valuable information.

'Everyone,' Roberto said with a helpless shrug, 'She would come to the gallery and sit and paint for hours. Many people would walk past, visitors and employees. Many would comment on her work, but I don't even think she heard them. It was like she was the only person in the room.'

Evie knew that she had only moments to decide whether to trust the young Italian. He had summed Alice up so well that Evie felt sure he knew her, not as a captive but as her usual free spirit.

Out of the corner of her eye she caught sight of a tall woman walking across the room they had recently left. As casually as she could, Evie turned so that her back was to the door. Roberto frowned, but made no comment.

'We think that she has been taken because of her art,' Evie whispered urgently. 'Our theory is that she is being forced to paint copies, and that these are being either sold or used to replace the real thing in galleries.'

Roberto nodded, and Evie was a little surprised that he didn't laugh. Even to her own ears it sounded far-fetched and more than a little ridiculous.

'There is a market,' he said. 'Private collectors. They do not wish to display their art to the world, it is for their own pleasure. They do not care if people visit a gallery to look at a copy. They are just content to know that they own the real painting.'

Evie risked a glance over her shoulder. The tall woman, who Evie felt certain was Elizabeth Sullivan, was now standing talking to a group of older men who seemed to hang on her every word. So much for Tom's reassurances that she would not be here! If Sullivan turned around, she would most likely see Evie.

'Do you have any idea who?' Evie said quickly, knowing that time could be running out for their conversation. Roberto looked thoughtful.

'It could be any number of organisations. It is a lucrative market.' Something seemed to cross his face and he was lost in thought.

'But you have your suspicions?'

'About the buyer? No. But there is someone who works at the gallery . . . ' His voice trailed off.

'Miss Spencer, may I ask what you are doing here?'

The tone was icy. Evie considered for a moment ignoring it, and trying to continue the charade that she was in fact Tom's sister, but she knew that voice and knew that she would not get away with it. Instead, she decided to try and brazen it out. She turned, fixing a smile on her face.

'Ms Sullivan. Lovely to see you again. May I say that your dress is simply stunning?' Evie surprised even herself; she sounded like she was an actress on a movie set and not Eve Spencer, accountant by day and homebody by night.

'You did not answer my question,' Ms Sullivan said, one eyebrow raised and a no-nonsense look on her face. Her makeup was immaculate and took years off her; only her hands gave an indication of her true age. In one hand she held a diamanté clutch, and in the other a glass of champagne.

'Well, I found a fellow art lover, and we were discussing what other galleries I should go and see.' Evie turned and indicated Roberto, but he was gone. Evie wasn't sure if she was relieved or concerned. Her general mistrust told her that she didn't want Roberto anywhere near Ms Sullivan or the rest of the representatives of the British government in Rome, but she was also desperate to find out what else he could tell her about the people involved in Alice's disappearance.

'I think you know that is not what I mean.' The impossibly plucked eyebrow moved even higher on the woman's face.

'I'm here as a guest,' Evie said, deciding to share as little information as possible.

'Of whom?' Ms Sullivan replied.

'Of me.' A warm voice sounded at her elbow, and Evie nearly jumped out of her skin as Tom seemed to materialise at her side from nowhere.

'Indeed,' Ms Sullivan said. Again Evie felt like a silent but heated conversation was going on but that she was not party to its meaning.

'If you will excuse me, Ms Sullivan; I have received a request from the Lady Ambassador, who wishes to speak to my sister.'

Without giving the older woman any chance to answer, Evie found herself swept away and back into the throng of the party.

'I'm guessing we are in trouble now?' Evie whispered into Tom's ear, keeping a smile on her face so as not to betray her true feelings to the Ambassador's wife, who they were heading towards.

'It was a calculated risk, and besides, Sullivan won't risk a scene here.'

Evie's thoughts were in a whirl. All she wanted to do now was to be able to tell Tom all that she had found out, and allow him to do the same with whatever he had come up with, but she knew better than to ask. They had a part to play, and she needed to play it. The Ambassador's wife held out a hand and Evie shook it, giving a deferential nod of her head and a warm smile — maybe she was better at this acting lark than she'd thought — and joined in the conversation about up-and-coming local artists.

Although Evie would probably never admit it out loud, she had almost enjoyed the evening. She had certainly met some interesting people, but nothing could distract her from her mission; and so, when Tom finally slipped his arm through hers, she couldn't help but feel relieved.

'Lady Ambassador, I'm afraid I must whisk my sister away. She has a plane to catch in the morning, and alas, her flight is intolerably early.'

'But of course. Lovely to meet you, Caroline,' the lady said, and with a nod she turned her attention to other guests. The clock on the wall told Evie that it was nearly midnight, and she had a sudden sense that she knew how Cinderella must have felt.

Evie didn't resist as Tom walked her through the hall crowded with visitors saying their goodbyes and preparing to leave. She was desperate to climb back into the car where they could talk and she could tell him what she had learned. They had to wait, of course, for their car to draw up to the main entrance; and when it did, Tom opened the door for her and waited for her to get in. It was a charming move, but Evie found it irritating in the circumstances, as it merely delayed their conversation for a few more seconds. When Tom had settled into the car beside her and given instructions to the driver, he turned to Evie.

'Not here,' he said. 'When we get home.'

Evie rolled her eyes in exasperation. There had never been an issue with them discussing Alice's case before. Her eyes drifted to the back of the driver's head; he, for his part, seemed focused on the job of navigating the streets, which were surprisingly busy considering the time of night. Evie moved her gaze back to Tom, who seemed deep in thought and oblivious to her presence. She made herself take a deep breath. It was probably a good sign. Surely it meant he had found some important — maybe crucial — information, and the only place he could safely share it was in the security of his apartment.

With Tom's gaze firmly fixed away

from her, Evie took advantage and studied him more closely than she had previously allowed herself. He was definitely handsome, and seemed at ease in his expensive suit. His eyes were a deep brown and seemed to give both nothing and everything away. She put him in his mid- to late thirties; as with most men, age seemed to refine his features and make him even more attractive and mysterious. Evie had sworn off men, having been disappointed one too many times. She'd found it hard to trust anyone before her first serious relationship, and since — well, she knew she defaulted to automatic distrust. She couldn't pin this feeling down, wondering if it was desperation to find Alice and to do whatever it took, even breaking her own personal rule to trust someone who she barely knew.

Evie was too lost in thought to realise that Tom's attention was now focused back on her. She blinked as she took in his gaze and the smile that was tugging at the edges of his mouth. Clearly, he had clocked her staring at him, and had drawn his own conclusions; like most men in Evie's experience.

'What?' she asked, a little crossly, before she could really think about it.

'Nothing,' he said innocently. 'I was just thinking that you were looking at me just now how I looked at you when I first saw you in that dress.'

Now Evie was nonplussed. She had expected some adolescent teasing — not what, to her ears, had sounded suspiciously like a declaration of feelings. She turned away to give herself a few moments to think. There was no way they could go down this road, not even a little. There was too much at stake: she needed Tom focused on finding Alice, not being distracted by her. Even the thought that he could like her in that way seemed impossible to Evie. She just wasn't the kind of woman that men fell for. No, she was misreading the situation. What was needed now was to return to the businesslike relationship that they had been used to.

'Anyone would look good in this dress,' she said with a wave of her hand, hoping that she was being suitably dismissive without appearing rude.

'I'm sure Valentina would be glad to hear that,' he replied, still sounding amused.

'I think we have more important things to discuss than our outfits, don't you?' Evie said, wincing at her own schoolteacher's tone.

'Indeed,' Tom said. There was no trace of amusement now. It was as if he had switched that part of his brain back to Government Agent with no apparent difficulty. 'But, as I said, not here.'

They travelled the remainder of the journey in silence. It wasn't the first time they had shared space and said nothing, but it was the first time that Evie had felt mildly uncomfortable. She knew that if Alice had been there, she would have soundly been told off for being rude and allowing the past to influence her future. But Alice wasn't there, and that was the problem.

The car pulled up outside the apartment block, and the driver got out and held open the door for her. Evie slid out as elegantly as she could. She had expected Tom to be there to hold her arm as she found her feet on her high heels, but he was striding away to the front door of the apartment complex, with merely a glance over his shoulder to check that she was following. Feeling more than a little put out, she reached for the shoulder of the driver to get her balance, and took her time pulling off her heels. Tom, for his part, had used his swipe card to open the main door and was now stood waiting for her. She padded barefoot across the pavement before turning and thanking the driver in her stilted Italian.

18

Evie couldn't believe the change she felt. She had been so desperate to talk to Tom, to find out what he knew and to share all that she had discovered, but now she felt a childish petulance fight for prominence. If he was going to behave like that, she didn't want to talk to him. She knew that she was being ridiculous, and these matters were far more important than her own ruffled feathers, but still. She decided to allow herself the short trip in the lift as sulking time.

Evie risked a quick glance at Tom, but either he was completely unaffected or was a great actor, since he showed no sign of any discomfort. A sigh escaped Evie's lips; there was really no point sulking if your target was oblivious. Tom glanced at her with an expression of mild interest, and Evie mentally shook herself. This sort of behaviour was not like her at all, and she needed to snap out of it. She manged a small smile and lifted up the pair of heels she held in her hand, as if to indicate that the sigh was due to sore feet rather than anything else. Tom nodded and then led the way out of the lift and into his apartment. Evie placed the shoes carefully on the floor; she had borrowed them from Valentina, and wanted to make sure they were returned in the same condition.

'Coffee?' Tom asked in a manner which suggested they had just been out for a quiet evening rather than on a reconnaissance mission. Evie forced herself to take a deep breath; if this was how he was going to play the game, then she would follow along.

'Yes please,' she said mildly before watching his reaction closely, wondering briefly if he was actually trying to get a rise out of her. He said nothing, but busied himself making coffee from scratch, which Evie had always considered a tad unnecessary and a little pretentious. When Tom had placed a cup of steaming coffee in front of her, she looked up expectantly.

'Am I to take it by your expression that you have come across a key titbit?'

Evie raised an eyebrow, despite her best efforts.

'A bit more than that, actually.'

Instead of showing any sign of being impressed, Tom merely nodded, appearing to Evie to be slightly distracted. She watched as he took a sip of coffee, and decided that she was done playing by his rules.

'I met Alice's boyfriend.' Evie hid her smile as she finally achieved a reaction from Tom, even though it was a frown.

'You didn't say Alice had a boyfriend.'

'I didn't know,' Evie replied.

Tom seemed to be adding this information to his internal files, so Evie decided to continue with her update.

'His name is Roberto, and he works at the Borghese Gallery, which is where he met Alice.'

Tom's face now showed concern and doubt, which Evie found irritating.

'What?'

'How do you know this man is Alice's boyfriend? He could have been anyone, Eve. I shouldn't have left you alone.' He shook his head now as if telling himself off.

'I was in the Ambassador's residence. How much danger could I be in?'

'The fact that you are asking that question would suggest you have no idea.' Tom's crossness seemed to have turned from himself to Evie.

'He told me things about Alice he would only know if he were close to her.'

Tom took another sip of coffee, and she could feel him study her face, which she worked hard to keep neutral.

'Like if he had held her captive for weeks.'

Evie could feel a small seed of doubt grow inside her but she pushed it down. If her childhood had taught her anything, it was that she had good instincts, and she wasn't about to start doubting herself now.

'He knew things about Alice and me.' Evie found herself talking slowly, as if she felt he wouldn't understand if she spoke quickly. 'I doubt very much Alice would be willing to share that kind of information with a stranger who had kidnapped her.'

''Kidnapping Victim 101',' Tom said, equally slowly, 'Ensure your captor starts to identify you as a human being. It means they will be more reluctant to hurt you.'

Evie clenched her teeth to bite back the retort she found so tempting to say out loud, but instead she said, 'You know that because presumably you have undergone some high-end training. My sister has not.'

'You don't need training, Eve. It's actually a natural human instinct to protect oneself.'

Evie slid off the stool and padded across the apartment. She needed to put some distance between herself and

Tom. His reaction to her information was starting to get beyond irritating, and her fatigue was making her feel like she might strike him. She stood staring out of the window at the street below, which was quiet at that time of night but still seemed to hold the magic of Rome.

'I'm sorry. I don't mean to upset you.' Tom's voice sounded from the seating area, and Evie turned; she hadn't even heard him move.

'I'm not upset,' Evie said, which was almost true. 'More like irritated that you don't seem to want to hear what I found out.'

Tom seemed to digest this, and then indicated with a wave of his hand that she should continue.

'Leaving the point as to whether Roberto is Alice's boyfriend or not — ' She paused, wondering whether Tom would reignite the argument; but he said nothing and appeared to be listening, so Evie continued.

'Roberto is a trainee art restorer and

evaluator. He has been away on a job, and was concerned when he hadn't heard anything from Alice. He said it was out of character, which I would have to agree with.'

Evie paused again and Tom nodded in agreement.

'He doesn't think she would have taken off any more than I do, at least not without telling us first. Then he told me how good Alice's reproductions were, and how openly she painted them in the gallery. He warned her to be careful, to be discreet, because she didn't know who was watching.'

Evie smiled inwardly. She was sure now that she not only had Tom's attention, but had also piqued his interest.

'He seemed to agree with your theory . . . ' Evie got no further as Tom interrupted her, his tone suddenly harsh.

'You told him?'

'No, of course not.' Evie said, making it clear she didn't appreciate the suggestion that she was so foolish. 'He merely put all the pieces together and came to the same conclusion as you.'

Evie paused and watched as some of the tension left his shoulders, but he was listening carefully now, and she couldn't help but feel vindicated for her response to his earlier dismissal of her news.

'He said he thought there were several organisations who could come up with that kind of plot.'

'Did he have any ideas as to who?'

Evie shook her head.

'No, but he seemed to think he might know someone at the gallery who could have noticed Alice, and who might have the right contacts.'

Tom was leaning forward now, both his coffee and pretence of only being mildly interested now long forgotten. Evie realised she was enjoying the moment a little too much when he snapped, 'Who?'

'I didn't get a chance to ask any more questions. That was when your Ms

Sullivan showed up.'

Tom stood up so fast that Evie started.

'Did she see you together?'

'Yes. I mean, it was awkward. She clearly wasn't expecting me to be there, and I guess she thought I had somehow managed to sneak in.'

Tom was striding across the room, and Evie stood, wondering what was going on.

'You need to get changed now.'

Evie looked down at the dress, thinking perhaps she had spilt something over the dress that had to go back to the store.

'Now, Eve. We need to leave right now. You have thirty seconds to put something more suitable on.'

Evie stood on the command, but she was confused. What on earth was going on? But one look at Tom's face told her that there was no time to explain, and so without a further thought she raced towards her room.

19

This time there was no chauffeured car waiting for them at the kerb. Instead, Tom pulled Evie by her hand out through the back of the apartment block. They wove their way through the service area and past the laundry room, through a fire door and into the back alley. Running past piles of black rubbish bags, Evie could now understand the urgency for her to get changed — there was no way she could have walked fast, let alone run, in those heels. She had so many questions burning through her mind, but she pushed them down. Now was not the time; whatever was happening, it was clearly very serious. So instead she focused her attention on Tom, half a step ahead of her and holding firmly to her left hand, and ordered her feet to keep up.

They bolted across main streets and then ducked back into shadowy alleys. In Evie's mind they seemed to be going in circles, but she knew that Tom must have some kind of plan. Occasionally she risked a look over her shoulder — she could see no sign that they were being followed, but Tom moved as if an army were close on their heels. Then he came to a halt so quickly that Evie didn't have time to adjust her pace, and so she barrelled into him. For his part, Tom seemed to have been expecting this, and had braced himself so that instead of taking them both down like a set of bowling pins, Evie found herself held tightly in his arms. The part of her brain that she was trying to ignore registered that it was more than happy to be held.

In another swift movement, Evie was spun round, and found herself crouched in the shadows of a sleek red car. She opened her mouth to try and catch her breath, but Tom seemed to think she was going to speak. He pulled her back into his arms with his hand preventing her from taking a deep breath, let alone talking out loud. She struggled briefly as her way of telling him that she wasn't happy about it, and then forced her body to relax. Tom had better things to be worried about than fighting to keep hold of her. His body felt tense beneath her, and she strained her eyes and ears to try and make out what danger he had detected, but there was nothing. The street was quiet at this early hour of the morning; even the party goers of Rome had found their way to bed.

Without a word, Tom was once again hauling her to her feet, and they were off. All Evie could make out as they ran past were silent run-down houses and small hotels that didn't look particularly welcoming. Evie was just getting to the point when she thought she was going to have to beg Tom to stop for a moment — her breathing was ragged and her chest burning — when he pulled her into a doorway on a tiny side street, and through a glass-fronted door that looked like it hadn't been cleaned for a couple of centuries.

Evie blinked as she adjusted to the low lighting, which still seemed bright to her eyes. They were in a small foyer and there was a glass-fronted service desk in front of them. An elderly man was sat behind the glass with a TV blaring out an Italian game show. Tom spoke quickly to him, handed over a pile of notes, and was handed a key on a rusted metal keyring. The elderly man didn't pause from his TV watching to even look at them; something that Evie couldn't help but feel grateful for. Tom led her through another door and up a rickety set of stairs to the top of the building before he used the key to unlock a room.

He held up a finger, which Evie took as a sign she should wait before speaking, and she watched as he quickly searched the room, which was basic in the extreme. Tom indicated that she should come in, and as soon as she had crossed the threshold he once again locked the door. He picked up the one wooden chair — which didn't look like it would hold a person's weight — and jammed it under the door handle. The room held one double bed that seemed to sag in the middle. It was covered with the kind of shiny bedspread that screamed both 'old' and 'well-washed'. There was no carpet on the floor except for a worn rug. A small table sat beside the bed, and held a lamp and a Bible. There was no sign of a door which led to a bathroom, so Evie could only assume that those kinds of facilities were shared. The thought made her shudder just a little, but at the same time she felt a sense of relief — surely no one would think to look for them here.

Tom stood by the window, which overlooked the small alley at the front of the hotel, and with one finger held aside the grey net curtains so he could complete his security survey. The minutes ticked by and Evie held her tongue, despite her desperate need to ask what was going on. She sat on the edge of the bed with her feet on the floor to stop the inevitable roll towards the middle of the mattress and waited. Finally, Tom seemed to remember that she was also in the room; either that, or he was satisfied that for now they were safe.

'Sorry about that,' he said mildly as if he had just turned up late for a dinner date.

'What's going on?' Evie asked, deciding to cut to the chase. 'I think we can trust Roberto.'

'It's not Roberto I'm worried about.'

Evie frowned. Tom seemed to change his mind a lot, since he had not an hour ago criticised her for talking to the man.

'I spoke to some contacts at the party, and I made a tentative connection that concerns me.'

Evie's eyes went wide.

'Ms Sullivan?' She couldn't believe it. Someone so high up in the Embassy. That sort of thing only happened in movies, didn't it?

Tom nodded grimly.

'At this point it remains tentative, but knowing that she saw you with a potential source of information . . . well, that concerns me.'

Evie took a moment to digest this.

'Do you think Roberto is in danger?' The thought made her heart constrict. Dragging one of Alice's friends into this was not what she had planned, and she cursed herself for not being more discreet. 'I should have arranged to meet him somewhere else. Somewhere we wouldn't be seen.'

'It's not your fault,' Tom said, and Evie looked up to see his gaze fixed upon her. 'In fact, the information you have could be vitally important. I suspected that someone connected to the Embassy might be involved, but it never occurred to me it could be my boss. If it's anyone's fault, it's mine.'

He turned away from her to look out of the window again, and Evie felt she knew him well enough to guess his thoughts. He was blaming himself, as if he was responsible for everyone's safety,

'Since you're not the master of the universe, I don't think you can blame yourself for not being able to control all possible events.'

He glanced at her, and she smiled.

'I know I haven't said it much, but I am grateful for all you are doing. I've been so focused on Alice I hadn't really considered any risks you might be taking with your own life and future.'

'I made the mistake of trusting her. I've worked with her for some time, and she seemed so dedicated to her job. I couldn't imagine her betraying that . . . '

'You have to trust some people,' Evie said, surprising both herself and Tom with her words.

'You seem to get by,' Tom said, and Evie felt there was a hint of amusement in his voice.

'And there I was thinking I kept that part of me well hidden.'

Tom smiled. 'I suspect you have plenty of experience that tells you not to.' His words were soft, but Evie knew they cut to the heart of the matter. She shrugged.

'There are some people in your life that you should be able to trust, but when they let you down, over and over again . . . they teach you a lesson that no child should have to learn.'

'I'm sorry.'

Evie tried a smile. The irony of the situation — that Tom had become the one person, other than Alice, that she had allowed in for most of her life — was not lost on her.

'Then situations happen, and you meet a person who makes you feel that perhaps that lesson doesn't need to apply to everyone.' Tom's eyes found hers and Evie felt like this was a man she could trust. They weren't just words, it was more powerful than that. Something inside her had changed. The voice of warning was still there, telling her to trust no one, but somehow it was being drowned out by something else, something stronger.

'Interesting that I have just experienced the opposite,' Tom said as he moved away from the window.

'Take my advice. Don't let one person who has let you down affect how you feel about every other person in the world. It makes for a lonely life.' Evie stared down at her hands. She had never said those words out loud, but she knew they were the truth. She hadn't let anyone near her for such a long while, and for the first time she had admitted both to herself and someone else that it didn't necessarily make life any better. Perhaps safer, but not better.

'I don't think I would have survived this without you,' she said softly. She was afraid to look up, afraid to see his reaction, which she was sure would form some kind of rejection. And she couldn't blame him. If nothing else, the circumstances they found themselves in were not conductive to more than taking the steps they needed to find Alice and survive the experience. But whatever it was that was burning inside her made her choose otherwise, and so she looked up. Tom had moved nearer, and when she looked up her eyes locked with his.

'You're not alone, Evie.' Tom's words were softly spoken and Evie could see a battle rage across his face, a fight of emotions, and she waited to see which one would triumph. Her head told her that the right thing would be to let the moment pass — Alice needed them to be fully focused on the task at hand — but her heart wanted something different. It was more than a want; it *needed* something else. Tom raised a hand and gently lifted her chin so that he could see her face more clearly.

'Right now we need to focus on staying safe and finding Alice.' She could see a trace of pleading in his eyes, and knew that he was desperate for her to understand that this was not a rejection; but Evie's heart had walked this path too many times in the past, and she could feel it start to close in on itself, as it always did to protect her.

'What's our next move?' she asked, unable to keep her usual businesslike tone from her voice and too scared to look to Tom for his reaction.

'It's a risk, but we need to make contact with Roberto.'

'Right,' Evie said, standing up.

'Not right now. Now we sleep. We'll go when the crowds are at their busiest tomorrow to create the best chance of cover.' With those words Tom turned away and took up his sentry position at the window. Not knowing what else to do, Evie rolled over and willed herself to sleep.

20

The noise outside woke Evie from her fitful sleep. The small side street was clearly a shortcut for all manner of businesses that delivered their wares early. Shouts in Italian, beeping car horns, and the sound of boxes being dropped onto the pavement filled the room. Evie sat up and her heart clenched in her chest as she scanned the room and realised she was alone. Tom was gone. It wasn't like there was anywhere in the tiny room for him to hide. Evie swung her legs out of bed and traced a path around the room anyway, needing to do something. Her thoughts went back to the conversation last night, and for a few heart-pounding moments she wondered if he had abandoned her.

In her initial panic, she had missed the torn-off piece of paper which had been carefully placed on the one bedside table. Evie practically ran to it, and just the sign of handwriting eased some of the fretting. She scanned it quickly: it told her very little. Tom had gone out for 'supplies' and would return shortly, whatever that meant. Evie could feel annoyance build inside her. Why hadn't he woken her up so they could go together? The annoyance quickly faded as the memory of their conversation replayed in her mind. Maybe he needed some space? She had certainly not made things easier between them. She cursed herself for not being more guarded — it was so unlike her, but the only thing she could put it down to was the fear and loss that she had experienced since Alice had disappeared.

The slight rattle of the door made her jump.

'It's me,' came a muffled voice, and then Evie heard the key turn in the lock. She had no way to tell whether it was Tom or someone else as the door was an effective sound barrier, so she scanned the room for some form of weapon. The only thing she could see was the lamp on the side table, and so she grabbed it; not bothering to waste valuable time unplugging it, she dragged it clean from its socket. The door opened and Evie raised the lamp over her head, ready to strike despite the shaking in her hands.

'Easy there. It's just me,' Tom said, managing to look both pleased that she was taking her personal safety seriously, and amused at her choice of weapon.

Evie felt the air inside her escape her lungs and it was like a balloon deflating. She felt behind her for the bed and sank down on to it. Tom was carrying two brown paper bags and looked as if he had been shopping.

'I have food and some outfits that will help us blend in,' he said, dumping them on the bed.

After they had eaten a breakfast of pastries and coffee, Tom handed Evie a bundle of grey cloth. Evie stared first at it and then at him. Tom shrugged.

'It's Rome; it's the perfect way to

hide in plain sight.'

Evie watched as he turned his back on her and pulled off his shirt, revealing his toned back. Realising she was staring, she turned away herself just in case Tom caught her in the act, and started to get changed. Two minutes later and their transformations were complete. Tom was dressed as a priest, complete with full-length black cassock and stole as well as the white dog-collar. Evie was now garbed as a nun in a long grey dress which reached her ankles, a white collar, and a crucifix on a long chain. She was just trying to work out how to put on the headgear when Tom stepped over.

'Here,' he said as he slipped it over her head and into place. Evie's mind wanted to ask how he knew how to do that, but it didn't seem the right time to distract with humour.

'Isn't this wrong?' Evie asked. Despite not being a churchgoer herself, it still felt faintly disrespectful.

'I told Father Antonio it was a matter

of life and death, and he handed them over without complaint. No doubt he is also praying for us, which I suspect we are in dire need of right now.'

Evie looked up sharply, wondering if he was mocking the priest, but there was no trace of that in his face — merely respect and understanding.

'I can see how this might help on the streets, but do you find many priests at art galleries?'

Tom smiled. 'Well, they will often come to look at the religious artwork, yes — but that's not where we are going.'

Evie opened her mouth to ask, but Tom was halfway across the room with a hand out to unlock the door; so instead she shrugged and followed him in a manner which she hoped reflected her new role.

They moved quickly from the side street on to the main thoroughfare. It was busy now, not so much with tourists but with ordinary Romans heading to work and school — or, for the most dedicated, to early-morning Mass. To

Evie's relief, no one gave them a second glance, and it was obvious that in Rome, at least, people dressed in religious vestments didn't warrant any additional attention. Tom walked with slow purpose, giving the impression that he had somewhere to be but with no need to hurry, and so Evie fell into step beside him. Tom smiled and nodded to people who greeted him with 'Good morning, Father,' and Evie followed his lead when people addressed her as 'Sister'.

They crossed a square whose main feature was an old church, just as the bell sounded the half-hour. As if on cue, the large wooden doors were thrown open; a priest in white vestments stepped out and began to say goodbye to the steady stream of parishioners. Evie followed Tom as he moved into the shadow of the steps that led up to the church, and there they waited. Evie had no idea what was going on or how this would help them find Roberto, but it didn't seem the time or place to ask that question.

The steady stream fell to a trickle, and the last few members said their goodbyes. A tall young man appeared on the steps and stood for a while in deep conversation with the priest. It was obvious from the gestures that he was seeking consolation or encouragement. It was then that Evie recognised him as the young man she had met at the Ambassador's party. She dragged her eyes from Roberto to stare in wonder at Tom. How on earth had he known that Roberto would be here — at this church, out of all the churches in Rome? Tom seemed aware of her gaze and smiled, all the while keeping his eyes fixed on Roberto.

'Father Antonio knows everything about everyone.'

Evie barely had time to process this new piece of information before Tom was stepping out of the shadows and walking towards the bottom of the steps. When he reached them he seemed to be unaware that Roberto was hurrying down the steps and they almost collided.

'Sorry, Father,' Roberto muttered distractedly in Italian. Tom waved the comment away and Evie stepped into view. Roberto nodded vaguely at her, and Evie knew that her disguise was enough to fool him.

'Roberto,' she said softly, 'it's Eve Spencer, Alice's sister. This is my friend Tom who is helping me look for her.'

Roberto looked startled and then scanned the square behind them as if looking for possible threats.

'No one has followed us,' Tom said, with a confidence that Evie wasn't sure she shared. 'We need to speak with you. Perhaps you could go back into the church as if you had forgotten something. We will come and find you there.'

Roberto hesitated for a split second and then nodded.

'Thank you, Father.' He made a show of having forgotten something, patting at his pockets, and then hurried back up the steps and into the church.

Tom nodded at Evie and they walked

off around the church before ducking through a side door. The church was ancient and beautiful, and Evie felt a sense of awe and peace. It was cool, and the air had the faint smell of incense. She followed Tom to a small side room, which, judging from the colourful pictures on the wall, was where the children had their Sunday school. Roberto was there, pacing up and down.

'Is there any news of Alice?' he asked, raking a hand through his hair.

'No, not yet,' Evie said reaching out a hand for his arm to comfort him.

'We are hoping you can help with that, Roberto,' Tom said in a tone which betrayed his businesslike manner, 'Eve seemed to think that you might know someone at the gallery who is connected.'

'You must understand, I am not sure,' Roberto said. 'I could be wrong, and the person of whom I speak is a good person. They would never willingly cause something like this to happen.'

'But?' Tom asked, clearly knowing that there was more to the story.

'But love for your child can make you do things that you would ordinarily not,' Roberto said, and this time he looked Tom firmly in the eyes as if he were weighing the other man's understanding. Tom nodded.

'We will be discreet. I'm not interested in punishing this man, merely finding Alice and getting her to safety.'

Roberto seemed relieved, and Evie could see some of the tension relax from his body. He had clearly been battling with a dilemma, and had been able to let go of at least some of it.

'His name is Pascal. He is a good man. He works as a cleaner. Works hard to keep his family, but his middle son . . . he is trouble.'

Tom nodded and Evie said nothing, not wanting to break the spell or give Roberto cause to keep what he knew to himself.

'His son is in deep. Has run up huge gambling debts with people you would want nothing to do with. Pascal has tried everything, *everything* to get him out of the life. It is just possible that he may have mentioned Alice's skill to someone who would use it for ill. Perhaps thinking he could buy favour for his son.'

Roberto turned to Evie.

'If he did this, he would have been desperate. He is a good man.'

Evie tried to force down the range of emotions, anger being at the forefront. She wanted to reassure Roberto that she understood. She certainly understood that fierceness of love that could force you to do anything to protect those that were your family; but to put a young woman in such a precarious situation — to put her little sister in that kind of situation — that would not be something she could easily forgive.

'I understand.' She forced the words out, partly to reassure Roberto but also because she could feel Tom's gaze on her, and she knew him well enough now to recognise when he needed her to do or say something. 'I don't want to punish Pascal, I just want Alice back safe.'

'As do I,' Roberto said, and Evie could see tears forming in his eyes but he abruptly brushed them away. 'What else can I do?'

'Nothing for now,' Tom said. 'We will approach Pascal discreetly at the gallery.' Roberto nodded.

'It is important that you give him no indication that we are coming, Roberto. We don't want to spook him. He may be being watched.'

'I would not risk Alice's life so.' The words were spat out in anger, and they made Evie take a step back, but Tom for his part seemed completely unruffled. He held Roberto's gaze and then, seemingly satisfied, said, 'Good.'

'Will you tell me when you find her?' Roberto asked, looking now to Evie.

'Of course,' Evie said, with a confidence that she wasn't sure was real. 'I suspect she will want to see you too.' She smiled but it wasn't returned.

'I should have kept her safe,' Roberto said, looking about as miserable as it was possible to be.

'You warned Alice?' Evie asked, wanting to take away some of his pain. Roberto nodded. 'Knowing my sister like I do, I suspect she ignored you.' Roberto nodded again. 'Roberto, I need you to hear this. This is not your fault.' There was a pause, and Evie could see the internal struggle going on inside him. When he finally nodded a third time, there were tears again, but this time he didn't bother to try and hide them. Evie pulled him into her arms.

'We're going to find her,' Evie promised him as much as she had fiercely promised herself. 'I promise.'

21

The gallery was bustling with tourists as Evie and Tom climbed the steps into the main foyer. Tom led them off to the stairs, which led to an upper floor where the bulk of the religious paintings were held.

'How will we know who Pascal is?' Evie asked quietly as she walked beside him.

'Everyone here wears photo ID. We will just have to pay close attention.'

A while later, Evie felt like she had studied every piece of artwork in the gallery. Her feet ached and so did her back. The slow walking and standing gazing at each piece seemed agonising; all her mind could do was think about where Alice was right now, and the fact that they seemed to be stuck staring at art when they should be doing something.

'I know this is frustrating, but try not to let it show,' Tom murmured as he moved to stand beside her and gaze at a painting of the parting of the Red Sea. Evie wanted to say something, but knew that Tom was doing what needed to be done.

'Maybe he's not even working today,' she suggested after several more minutes had passed.

'I got the impression from our friend that money was tight. If that is the case, he is bound to be at work at some point today.'

They moved out into the main corridor. A door that had been previously invisible from the outside opened, and a man in a janitor's uniform walked out backwards, pulling a cleaning trolley behind him. Evie started forward, but felt Tom's restraining hand on her arm. She watched as he scanned the other visitors, and then, presumably feeling it was safe, he stepped forward as if he was heading to one of the other rooms. He passed the man and greeted him in Italian. Evie knew enough to understand that this was not Pascal, but couldn't follow the rest of the conversation. She waited, pretending to be engrossed in a small statue which sat on a plinth, and waited for Tom to make his way back.

'He's working in the basement today, where the restaurant is,' Tom murmured, as if he were merely passing comment on the weather; and then he strolled off, again looking as if he had no other purpose than to admire the treasures that the gallery held.

Once at the restaurant, Tom found them a table which gave a clear view of the rest of the diners, and ordered two coffees and open sandwiches. Evie raised an eyebrow.

'Even priests have to eat,' he said with a shrug.

But Evie was not paying attention. Another man in a janitor's uniform had appeared, pushing along a mop and bucket. Tom followed Evie's stare.

'Wait here.'

Evie opened her mouth to argue, but Tom held up a hand, looking as if he were about to give her a blessing. 'It will draw less attention if I speak to him alone.'

Evie wanted to argue, but she knew that Tom was right, so nodded and offered no further argument. She tried not to follow Tom's every step with her eyes, and forced herself to look around as if she were taking in the vaulted ceilings and tapestries that hung on the wall. She was surrounded by tourists in t-shirts and shorts, heavily laden with cameras, and with bags indicating they had visited the gallery shop. One couple stood out, though — everyone else seemed engrossed in conversation, but they seemed watchful. Evie looked down and took another sip of her coffee before casually looking up. There it was again: just a glance, but it lingered too long. Evie knew something was wrong. Everyone else had paid her and Tom little or no attention. The sight of people from religious orders was commonplace in Italy.

Evie risked another glance, and this time caught the woman's eye. Slowly, Evie stood and started to walk towards the exit, away from where Tom was talking quietly to Pascal. She wasn't sure what she was hoping to achieve. Perhaps they hadn't seen Tom, perhaps they hadn't realised who he was talking to. It all seemed unlikely, but perhaps she could draw them away to allow Tom enough time to find out what they needed to know.

Once she reached the archway which led to the stairs, she bolted. The scene of a running nun clearly did draw people's attention, and Evie could hear startled comments and exclamations as she took the stairs two at a time.

At the top of the stairs there was a set of large glass doors. Evie pushed through them and found herself in a sea of people in the main foyer. She weaved in and out, aware now that she had captured the attention of at least one part of the team who she was sure was there to follow them. The woman burst through the doors, admittedly making less of a scene than Evie in her nun's garb, but drawing eyes nonetheless. Evie made a split-second choice to head for the exit. She might have been able to lose her foe for a while in the gallery, but what she needed was to put distance between her and Tom.

Once outside she slowed to a walk. There were people milling around on the steps and some were sitting down. The woman slowed too, clearly happy for now to keep her in eyesight rather than risk a direct attack in such a public place. Evie moved carefully, keeping an eye open for any accomplices.

Her feet faltered as she saw a large black car drive up at the foot of the steps. A man stepped out, dressed in sunglasses and a dark suit. He took the time to button his jacket before opening the rear door. Evie blinked. She was sure that what she was seeing wasn't real, that her mind was playing tricks on her. That she wanted to see Alice so badly that she was now seeing visions of her.

'Evie!' The shout was enough for Evie. Now she knew. She would recognise that voice anywhere. She started to run down the steps and towards the kerb where the car was parked.

'No!'

Evie faltered and nearly missed a step as she heard a cry from a different direction. The man in the suit stepped towards Evie, and all she could think of was Alice, being with Alice, even if that meant being captured herself. If she was with Alice, she could protect her as she had always done.

'Evie! No!' This shout was definitely not Alice, and she turned her head as she ran to see Tom racing towards her. The man in the suit looked from Evie to Tom and put a finger to his ear, clearly receiving instructions from someone. In one swift movement he was closing the car door, and Evie could no longer see Alice. She cried out in a cross between a scream and a wail, but the man ignored her and merely climbed back into the front seat. As Tom's arms grabbed hold of her, the engine turned over and the car burned rubber as it screeched down the street.

'Let go of me!' Evie managed to force the words out between sobs, but the arms didn't let her go; instead, she felt herself pulled into a tight embrace.

'I'm sorry,' Tom said. 'We need to move — now. It's not safe here, and we are attracting too much attention.'

The only word that Evie could say was 'Alice,' and then those strong arms were dragging her down the street and away from the gallery. Evie's legs didn't seem to want to hold her weight, and so Tom slipped an arm around her waist and half-carried, half-dragged her down a quiet side street.

'Evie, Evie!' Tom said. 'I need you to focus, we have to get out of here.' His tone was urgent in a way that she hadn't heard from him before, but she wasn't sure that she cared. She had been so close to Alice, she could have reached out and touched her, but once again she was gone, taken away from her by men who might mean her harm.

'Evie!' This time she could feel herself being shaken, and her teeth chattered. 'I know where she is. I know where Alice is.'

Evie felt as if she had just touched a live wire. The sentence seemed to travel through her like electricity, and her mind came back into sharp focus. Her knees steadied and she shook herself free from Tom's grip. There was only one word she needed to say.

'Where?'

'Not here.'

Evie shook her head. She wasn't going to take another step until she knew where Alice was.

'Trust me,' Tom said and he looked at her until she made eye contact. 'Trust me now, Evie, we are so close. But we can't do this here, not after what has just happened.'

Evie didn't trust herself to speak. She merely nodded and allowed Tom to grab her hand and lead her away.

The last place she expected to find herself was back at the run-down hotel, but that was where their circuitous path had led them. The adrenaline she had felt was starting to wear off, and fatigue was starting to set in. She followed Tom back up the staircase to the room which she was currently calling home, and pulled off the headgear which covered her hair.

22

Evie could feel the adrenaline start to fade and her body was sending her signals of exhaustion. She could feel herself start to shake. She had been so close, closer to Alice than she had been since she waved her off at the airport in London, but she had once again been swept away. The sensible part of her brain told her that Tom was right — getting captured would not help to free Alice — but her heart told her that she didn't care. She wanted to be with Alice, to hold her in her arms, whatever the circumstances. The emotions waged a war inside her and she followed Tom back inside the hotel room.

She turned her angry gaze on him. 'You should have let me go.'

'Evie,' he said slowly, and he was clearly choosing his words carefully, 'there had to have been a reason for them bringing Alice out in the open. They wanted her to see you, possibly so they could threaten her with your life. If you had gone with them, it would have only made that job easier.'

Evie felt all the fight leave her, and she stumbled towards the bed before allowing her legs to fold under her.

'Why would they need to threaten her?' Evie asked, her voice sounding hollow in her ears.

'Maybe they want her to do something, paint something, and she has been resisting.' Tom shook his head to suggest he didn't know. 'It's possible they are just doing it to keep her in line.'

He seemed lost in that thought, and Evie wondered if his mind were coming up with the same dire scenarios that hers was.

'We have to get her back.' Evie said the words softly and she knew she was begging. Whether she was begging Tom or a higher power, she wasn't sure.

'We will.' Tom's words were convincing, as if he knew for certain that they would. Evie looked up at him and he moved to stand in front of her.

'I promise, Evie. I know where she is and I'm going to get her.' There was a fierceness to his voice that she hadn't heard before.

'When do we leave?' Evie said, standing up and scanning the room for the clothes she had exchanged earlier for the nun's habit.

She felt Tom's hands on her arms and she looked down. She knew what that meant.

'Don't say it,' she said. 'I'm coming with you.'

Tom stared at her for what felt like an hour, and she held his gaze but had to fight not to get lost in it. She knew if she did she would agree to anything he said.

'It's too dangerous,' he said softly. He seemed to be holding himself rigidly, and Evie wondered if he was as desperate to fold her into his arms as she was to be held.

'It's Alice,' she replied simply, as if

that would explain it all.

Tom smiled now; it was a small smile, not one that Evie had seen before, and she thought her mind might be playing tricks on her as she felt the affection held within it.

'That's the problem, Evie. I know you would do anything to get Alice back, and that makes you kind of dangerous.'

Evie blinked.

'It's not meant as a criticism.' Tom smiled again and Evie knew that he meant what he was saying. 'It's actually one of the things I love about you.'

Evie thought her legs were going to give way beneath her. Tom obviously had seen that too, and he closed the gap between them and drew her into his arms. They stood there and just held each other, as if no words could sum up what they were both feeling in that moment. Evie tucked her head under his chin and listened to Tom's heart beat in his chest.

'I'm still coming with you,' she

whispered into his cassock. She both felt and heard his deep sigh.

'Evie, I need to focus on the job in hand. I can't be worrying about what you might be do.'

With some reluctance, Evie wriggled herself free from his grip and took a step back.

'Probably better to have me by your side, then,' she said, and raised both eyebrows. 'At least there you can keep an eye on me.'

Evie knew she was being unfair, although part of her thought they were both using the same tactics to get what they wanted.

'I'm not just going to stay here like a good little girl and wait for you to rescue my sister.'

Tom turned away from her, and she knew that he was trying to figure out whether she would follow through on her threat. She felt a pang of guilt, knowing that she was manipulating him, but also knowing that she couldn't let him put himself in danger for her without taking the same risks herself. He turned and opened his mouth to speak, but Evie got there first.

'It's not just Alice I'm worried about,' Evie said, and sought out his eyes. She needed him to understand. 'You have done so much for me, risked so much. I can't ask you to take on even more, unless I'm prepared to do the same.'

She watched as he ran his hand through his hair, still dressed in his priest's garb. It almost made her laugh out loud.

'No, Evie. I won't put you in danger.'

'It seems to me that I'm already there,' Evie said evenly. 'Leaving me here on my own seems pretty dangerous, too.'

Tom shook his head at her.

'You know you are trifling with my emotions, right?'

Now Evie did laugh; she couldn't help it. She shrugged.

'And you weren't doing the same with me?'

Tom had the good grace to look a little guilty.

'I love you.' The words were out of Evie's mouth before she could stop them. They had been floating around in her head for days, but it was not something she had consciously decided to say out loud. She put her hand to her mouth to prevent anything else escaping. Evie had always kept her emotions in check, and had certainly never been the first person to say the 'L' word. She could feel the panic whirling inside her, and knew she needed to put some space between them. Now was not the time, she knew, and in three foolish words she might have destroyed something which could have changed her life. She moved towards the window, away from him, and tried to pull back the emotions that threatened to overwhelm her. She was going to cry — more than that, she was going to sob. She was going to feel sorry for herself, but worst of all, she had lost sight of what this was really all about — Alice.

Before she could force the feelings down, she was pulled into Tom's arms again.

'I love you too,' he said; then she felt his body go tense and she was being pushed to the floor. 'Get down!' His voice sounded harsh and close, and she could feel his arm around her back, holding her down. She opened her mouth to speak but he put his finger to his lips as the sound of loud conversation floated up the stairs. Evie watched as his eyes scanned the room. What he was looking for, she couldn't tell. The only way out was the door to the room, which led on to the main stairs, and she could hear heavy footfalls. Her heart started to beat fast; they were so close to getting Alice back. They knew where she was, and now she had thrown it away by distracting Tom from his mission. She cursed herself even though she knew that wouldn't help, and tried to think of a way out.

Her eyes travelled to the window. They were on the top floor, three floors up. It was crazy, but it might be their only chance. She looked at Tom, and it was clear that he was thinking the same. He motioned for her to stay where she was, and then he belly-crawled over to the window. In an expert move, he lifted his head above the sill for a split second and then ducked back down. He held up one finger, which Evie took to mean there was one person outside. They sound of banging doors was getting closer. They had no time. Evie and Tom exchanged no words but they were in agreement.

Tom stood and Evie scrabbled for her feet. He opened the window and repeated his swift survey. Using both his hands, he demonstrated a motion which Evie could only interpret as climbing down something. She moved to join him at the window and tried not to let the fear show. It was a long way down to the street below, and there was nothing that could break their fall. Tom's glance moved to the black cast-iron drainpipe with rusted bolts.

He shook his head and gestured for her to look to the left.

Evie felt a little of the fear leave her, but only a little. To the left and one floor down was a small balcony. If she could climb down one floor, then she might be able to reach across and haul herself on to it. The fear was making her legs shake, but she forced them to obey her. There was too much at stake — not just her life and Tom's, the man she had come to love, but also Alice. Always Alice. And so she clambered through the now-open window and reached for the drainpipe.

23

The drain pipe felt slick beneath her fingers, and she knew if she hesitated she would not be able to force her fear-laden limbs to function. She could feel Tom's grip on her back, but knew she had to let go of that one tiny piece of security. With gritted teeth and an image of Alice in her head she lunged forward, grasping the drainpipe now with both hands, and feeling Tom let go. She closed her eyes and swallowed as the metal creaking noise seemed to radiate in her ears. She seemed frozen in time, knowing she needed to do something but not able to command her body.

'Evie, move!' Tom hissed, and there was the sound of splintering wood behind her. One look up at his face seemed to have the desired effect. She didn't know how she did it, but she managed to move little by little down towards the street, and nearer and nearer to the balcony of the building next door. A glance above told her that Tom was moving out of the window too, but he hesitated, clearly uncertain that the pipe would hold both their weight. Evie turned her attention to the railing of the balcony and reached out, skimming it with her fingertips. With an inward howl of frustration she moved so that she was gripping the drainpipe with only one hand and one leg, and leaned. This time her hand made contact with the railing, but she knew that she was going to have to let go of the pipe and trust that her right hand could take her full weight.

Think about Tom! she told herself firmly, and then swung herself across, making a grab for the railing. For a split second she felt like she was suspended in mid-air, and that at any moment she would find herself falling. Her fingers tightened their grip and held, despite the screaming from her shoulder. Her forward momentum made her swing, and she had to use the last of her energy to prevent herself from crashing into the side of the building. She reached up with her other hand and allowed herself a moment to catch her breath. Above her, Tom was making the move down the pipe look easy, and was gaining on her fast. She hauled herself up so that she had both arms over the side of the railings. Then, able to get purchase with one foot, she heaved herself over and fell in a crumpled mess onto the balcony floor.

Evie had time to take two gasps of breath before Tom's feet appeared beside her and she was being hauled to her feet. He picked up a small terracotta plant pot and used it to smash the glass near to the handle of the balcony door. Evie shielded her eyes and then followed him into the empty apartment. It reflected the hotel next door, containing a mismatch of furniture and worn furnishings. Evie scanned the room for a place to hide, but realised that Tom was heading towards the door. He listened for a moment and then yanked the door open. The bare corridor had creaky wooden floorboards and a set of stairs that ran upwards and downwards. Without a moment's hesitation, Tom grabbed her hand and they were soon taking the stairs up to the next floor, two at a time. On the next floor an elderly man in a black suit shuffled out of his door, and Tom and Evie had to take evasive action, running with their backs hard up against the staircase rail behind them.

Tom pushed open a door which didn't have a number on it and they found themselves racing up another staircase which would lead them to the roof. The roof was littered with old, unwanted furniture and evidence that the residents used the area as an impromptu outdoor area. There were water tanks on the roof, and Tom pulled Evie down behind one, then scrambled over the edge of the roof to check on their foe. Evie watched as he completed his quick scan then returned to her side.

'Is it the men that have Alice?' she asked quietly. Tom shook his head and then turned to her.

'The Federal Police.'

Evie frowned. Surely they shouldn't be running from them — maybe they could help? Then she remembered Tom's concerns that they couldn't be trusted.

'And some of my men from the Embassy.'

Now Evie's blood ran cold.

'Sullivan?' Her voice sounded scratchy, like she was having trouble saying the name. Tom nodded.

'But if they are your men, if you explain what is going on . . . ' Evie's voice trailed off as she saw the expression on his face.

'I don't know what *is* going on. I have no real proof of anything right now.'

There was more noise from the street below; the words were Italian, but Evie was sure they were instructions.

'We need to move,' Tom said before grabbing her hand and leading her across the roof.

Evie felt like they had been running and hiding for days, but it was probably not more than an hour. The nun's habit was heavy and hot and not designed for such activities. She had also removed her headgear, something a real nun would never do, and knew that it would likely attract unwanted attention. After some time, Tom had led her through another door, back down into a building and out on to the street. He let go of her hand then. Evie knew he needed to. A nun without her veil was a curiosity, but a nun holding hands with a priest would be a scandal. Her breath was almost painful in her chest now, and her cheeks were flushed as sweat pooled at her hair line. She looked a state and she knew it.

'In here,' Tom said, and grabbed her by the elbow, pulling her into a fenced-off area of a building that was being renovated. The whole front of the building was covered with scaffolding and plastic green mesh, presumably to stop any masonry falling on to the street below. Inside was dark and smelt of damp: clearly the renovations were in the early stages. The building was still, though, which gave the impression it was empty. Evie took this as a sign she could start to ask questions.

'Now what?' was all she could manage before she could recover from their extended run.

'Now we wait.'

Evie sighed.

'Wait for what?'

'For it to get dark. Then — ' He turned to face her. ' — we go and get Alice.'

Evie couldn't help but be startled by that revelation. After all, it didn't seem much of a plan. Not that Tom had had much time for such things, but as desperate as she was to hold Alice in her arms again, she knew that it wouldn't be easy.

'Okay,' she said, but her voice must have betrayed her uncertainty.

'There is someone I can trust, someone who can help us, but I need to

241

make contact with her.'

Evie nodded, digesting this last piece of information.

'I need you to stay here while I do.'

Evie held his gaze and didn't look away. She could detect no signs that he was planning on breaking his word and leaving her behind whilst he rescued Alice alone.

She swallowed down the memories that surfaced of times those she had trusted had let her down.

'I trust you.'

Now it was Tom's turn to fall silent, and his face registered that he knew how hard those words were for her to say. He reached out for her hand and gave it a squeeze. He then glanced at his watch.

'I'll be back within two hours.' He looked back at her, 'If I'm not, then I need you to promise me something.'

Evie frowned. What did he mean, if he wasn't back?

'If something happens, I need you to go back to the Embassy.'

Evie shook her head vehemently, both at the thought of him not coming back, but also the thought of going back to the Embassy, to Sullivan who had betrayed them.

'Not to Sullivan,' he said quickly, 'Ask to speak to the Ambassador's wife. Say that you have a message from the Saint Helene charity.'

'I don't . . . ' she started to say.

'Evie, the Ambassador's wife is ex-M15. I worked for her. I trust her, and so can you. That message is a code that only she and I share. She will protect you.'

24

Evie stared at the watch in her hand, willing it for once to slow down or maybe even start to run backwards. One thing she knew for certain but had been trying to ignore was the fact that the two hours had been up more than fifteen minutes ago. Evie felt paralysed by the fear. Did it mean that something bad had happened to Tom? Her sensible mind reminded her that this was not some blockbuster movie, and that in all probability it had simply taken Tom longer to contact his friend than he had expected. However, a small part of her, one that was so familiar it was hard to ignore, told her that he had betrayed her. That warning voice which she had always found as such a comfort was now only bringing her pain. What if Tom had gone to rescue Alice without her? What if he had broken his promise to her?

Evie had been pacing up and down for what felt like an age; her shoes had traced a path through the dust-covered floor, and she focused her mind on continuing to follow it. She was so used to knowing what the right thing was to do at any time that she felt lost. She had trusted Tom, and now he had either broken that trust or got himself captured — or worse. She clenched her fists, knowing she needed to stop obsessing and make a decision. Whatever had happened to Tom, he had told her what to do if he didn't make it back. She had a choice, of course, she could decide not to trust him, but then in truth she wasn't sure what she should do next. She had no idea where Alice was, no idea where Tom had gone, and no plan.

Evie walked towards the door and peeked out, but all she could see was the fencing that encircled the building. Her head and her heart were battling it out. Her heart told her to trust Tom, that her feelings were both real and reciprocated. If he hadn't come back, then she should follow his last instruction. Her head was still stuck in the past, showing her mind a collection of all the times that people she should have been able to trust had let her down.

'Enough!' she told herself crossly. 'You have to make a decision.' It was in that moment that Evie knew her heart had won. It was a risk, but it was one that she was going to take. Her head had been controlling her life for years, and where had it got her? She hadn't been hurt again, but her life had shrunk inwards until it really consisted of only her and Alice. Surely contacting the one person Tom said he could trust was the best way that Evie could help Alice and him.

Now she had a destination, she just needed to work out how to get there. She had no money, and no idea where she was in the labyrinth that was Rome. She would just have to walk until she reached an area that she recognised and work it out from there.

She peeked once again through the hole in the wire fence. The sun was starting to set and the street outside was bathed in a warm glow and deep shadow. There were few people about: the other building sites had emptied out, and everyone else seemed to be walking with purpose. Evie looked down at her nun's habit and tried to brush off the accumulated dust and various other stains she had gathered during their balcony leap and escape. She looked a sight, but hoped that no one would notice if she kept to the shadows. She had no veil either, which might draw a few curious gazes, but there was nothing she could do about that now.

Holding her breath, she squeezed through the gap with difficulty, and crouched low, allowing herself to scan the street one more time. She felt both scared and ridiculous, since she wasn't sure that she would recognise danger if she saw it. Then, taking a deep breath, she stood up and stepped out onto the street. In her mind, she tried to replay the route they had taken a few hours earlier, but she had to admit that memorising it had not been a top priority and the streets looked different in the low light. She could hear cars and traffic to her left and decided to head in that direction. Perhaps on a main road she could find her bearings.

Evie ignored the few curious glances that were sent her way, and kept her head down until she reached the road. It wasn't exactly busy, but it was better lit than the side streets, and she paused before a sleek black limo drove past. With no better hint to work off, she headed in the direction that it was travelling, reasoning that at this time in the early evening it was most likely headed towards the centre than away from it. With purpose now she sped up, focusing her jangled nerves on taking steps towards finding Alice and Tom.

The streets grew busy and Evie started to pass the small boutique shops that seemed to surround the outer streets of Rome. The number of curious stares increased, but Evie kept moving. Her feet started to ache and she was desperately thirsty, but she knew there was nothing to be done about that. A car slowed at the kerb and Evie braced herself to run. A man in a black tuxedo climbed out, and Evie's eyes went wide, but he ignored her — she doubted he had even seen her — and instead crossed in front of her to a cash machine in the wall of what Evie realised was a bank.

Evie could feel her face burn with embarrassment. How had she managed to get so paranoid that everyone appeared to be a threat? She shook her head and stumbled as she walked into a person moving in the opposite direction.

'Sorry,' she said, unable to grasp the correct word in Italian. She felt hands firm on each arm. At first she thought they were there to prevent her from falling, but the grip was too tight and lasting too long. She looked up and tried to slow her racing heart.

'It's okay, it's me,' the voice said. English, but with a heavy Italian accent. Evie looked up into the face of the about the only person other than Tom that she would have been happy to see in that moment.

'Roberto? What are you doing here? How did you find me?'

'Tom,' he said simply, his mouth set in a grim line. 'But we cannot talk here. Come with me.'

Roberto started to move off in the direction that Evie had already chosen. She fell into step beside him but kept her eyes on the people walking past, looking for signs of danger. Roberto seemed to know where he was going, but Evie still didn't see anything that she recognised.

'Are we going to the Embassy?' Evie asked quietly.

Roberto looked at her with a warning which made it clear that he didn't want to speak about it, and shook his head.

Evie's pace faltered. If Roberto had spoken to Tom, then surely Tom would have told him to take her there, take her to the one person he had felt sure he could still trust.

'What did Tom say?' Evie said, stopping now. Her inner sense of distrust was brewing. The events of the last few days had made her doubt whether it was her friend or her foe, but somehow she couldn't ignore it.

'Not here,' Roberto hissed, and now he seemed both angry and desperate.

'I'm not going another step until you tell me what is going on.' Evie dragged her eyes away from her visual survey for any signs of danger, and forced herself to focus on Roberto's face — she needed to see his reaction.

'Please,' he said, and Evie could see fear and something else in his eyes. 'We have to go.'

'Go where?' Evie asked as Roberto looked around, panic oozing out of every part of him.

'For Alice, we have to go!' He was

shouting now and drawing the attention of people walking past, who looked at him curiously, arguing as he was with a woman in a torn nun's habit.

'Roberto, I need to know what is going on.'

But Roberto was listening, he had a hand raised in the air, and was looking over Evie's shoulder. She turned but it was too late. A man was a few steps behind her, and before she could react had grabbed her firmly by the arms.

'I'm sorry,' Roberto said, and he looked it, looked desperate and unsure of himself as Evie found herself bundled towards a car which had pulled up at the kerb. The man instructed her to do something in Italian, but she didn't understand, so looked to Roberto.

'You have to get in,' Roberto said.

The grip on Evie's arm told her she had no choice, and so she climbed into the car and watched through the window as they sped away, leaving Roberto standing alone on the street.

25

Evie was sliding around in the back of the car as it sped through the winding streets. She reached up for the handle over the door to steady herself and tried to work out what she should be doing — or, better, what Tom would do in this situation. Roberto had betrayed them, but whether it was for money or from fear, Evie wasn't sure. What she did know was that Tom hadn't sent him, which brought more questions and more fear as to what had happened to Tom. She shook her head to try and focus. She needed to think. She needed a plan.

Evie tried to keep a mental note of landmarks they passed, but it quickly became a blur. The men in the car talked little to each other, but one of them had had a short and terse conversation on his mobile. Evie's

Italian wasn't up to translating any of what had been said. The car slowed and there was a beeping noise as it drove through a set of automated gates, down a short drive, and into a garage, whose door closed swiftly behind them.

Evie's door was opened, and an arm reached in and hauled her out. She just about managed to find her feet before she was hauled through another door and into what looked like a cellar. Unlike other cellars she had been in recently, this one was dust-free, used as storage for a variety of furniture covered in white sheets, but she was bundled on through another door before she could see anything else.

They crossed a hall to another door but this one had a man guarding it. He took little notice of Evie but was focused on her taciturn companion, who nodded, and the man hurried to unlock the door. He pushed the door open and before Evie had a chance to do anything she found herself flung into the room, turning just in time to see the door slammed shut and the sound of keys locking it firmly shut. Evie hit the floor hard and was just struggling to her knees when she found hands flung tightly around her neck. As the grip tightened she tried to pull away, and her head was filled with nothing but blind panic until, with a start, she realised someone was speaking to her, speaking to her in English.

'Evie? Oh, Evie! Are you okay?'

It took only a heartbeat for Evie to register whose voice she could hear. It was one that she had dreamed about, that she had longed for, and now she was hearing it, hearing her. Her eyes were sending her all sorts of other pieces of information — strawberry blonde hair, with a careless curl — and Evie just knew, without needing to stand back and look.

'Alice!' Evie wasn't sure if she had shouted or whispered her name, but she didn't care. Here was Alice, here in her arms, safe and well. The sensible part of Evie's brain reminded her firmly that they were anything but safe, but for that moment she didn't care. Evie held her little sister close and time seemed to be suspended. But after a while the need to know how Alice was, what had happened to her, was too great, and so Evie pulled back but still gripped her sister's shoulders.

'Are you okay? Did they hurt you?' Evie asked, feeling a lump of fear and dread build in her throat and catch at her eyes where tears threatened.

Alice shook her head.

'I'm okay. They haven't hurt me, they need me.' Alice shrugged in the way a person might when an event in their life had been so huge that they simply couldn't put it into words. Evie's eyes swept her sister from head to toe, needing more confirmation.

'Really, I'm fine,' Alice said, and Evie detected the all-too-familiar eye-roll that Alice would employ when Evie was what she called 'fussing'. Normally it would wind Evie up, but right now she could sit and watch Alice roll her eyes a million times.

'I need to tell you what is going on,' Alice said urgently, with one eye on the door. 'And you need to tell me what you know.

'What?' she added, suddenly suspicious, when Evie didn't answer. All that Evie could think about was how she was going to break the news of Roberto's betrayal. Alice took hold of her older sister's hand and pulled her towards an aged chaise longue. They settled down on it side by side, and Evie noted that Alice had not let go of her hand.

'It's such a long story I don't really know where to start,' Evie said, knowing she was playing for time.

'Well since neither of us has anywhere else to be, why don't you start at the beginning?'

Evie didn't think she had ever talked for so long with pausing for breath. She had to be careful, of course, for she had no idea who was listening, so she didn't mention anyone by name but simply told the story, relaying it as one might a bedtime story to a small child. Alice for her part seemed content to sit and listen, merely nodding and raising eyebrows at her older sister's adventures.

'And so I was making my way to the Embassy, or at least trying to, when I . . .'

Alice tilted her head to one side.

'You may as well just tell me. It can't be worse than being kidnapped and forced to copy great works of art,' Alice said dryly in that way she had. Taking in Evie's expression, she said, 'Whatever it is, you can tell me.'

Evie swallowed, reluctant to utter words that would break her sister's heart. Alice had always been trusting, had remained fiercely sure of who she could trust. It was something that Evie has always been a little jealous of — not in a bad way, more of an admiring one. Despite their experiences, Alice had managed to keep that part of herself unaffected. She didn't want to be the person who shattered that illusion.

'I met Roberto before I could get to the Embassy.'

Alice froze and Evie squeezed her hand.

'Have they hurt him?' There was such fear in her voice that Evie could feel the pain that thought had caused her. She pulled her sister into a one-armed hug.

'No. Roberto is fine.' Evie found it hard to say the word. He *was* fine — no doubt he had been handsomely rewarded for his treacherous actions. 'Alice, he told them where to find me. He said he was taking me somewhere safe, but really he was letting them know where to find me . . . '

Evie's voice trailed off as she could feel her sister shaking her head.

'Evie, I asked them to find you. We tried at the gallery that day, but when that didn't work, they said they would have to find someone who could help them. I guess they meant Roberto,' she said simply, and to Evie's surprise there was no anger or uncertainty in her voice. Alice had spoken as if it were a fact, like the sky being blue.

'But Alice, I'm sorry, but he isn't who you think he is.'

Evie was sure that what Roberto had done was for money and not for his love of Alice.

Alice wriggled out of her arms and moved around so that she was sitting cross-legged and facing her sister.

'I trust him. They probably told him what was going on. Probably said that I wanted you here.'

Evie ran a hand through her hair. She had been so certain that she knew what was going on, but none of what Alice said was making any sense. She wanted to scream at Alice, and then she wanted to tell her that it was okay because they had each other and they didn't need any-one else, but she couldn't seem to find the way to put that sentiment into words.

'I knew it!' Alice said bouncing up and down beside her.

Evie stared, wondering if the kidnap-ping had taken a greater toll than she had thought.

'Alice, calm down. I know that this is a shock to you and all that, but . . . '

Alice was flapping her hands and waving off Evie's comments.

'Not that,' she said dramatically, and Evie felt like she was reliving Alice's teenage years. 'It's that guy, isn't it?'

Evie tried to act confused. She of course knew exactly who Alice was referring to, but couldn't imagine any time less suitable for this conversation, even though a big part of her was dying to talk to Alice about him, about Tom. His presence in her life had been a revelation, and she knew she had changed because of it, but now was most definitely not the time to talk about it, particularly if anyone was bothering to listen to them.

'Not a topic for right now,' Evie said and tried to convey her meaning in her expression, but Alice was too far gone to care. She had stood up and was starting to hop from foot to foot.

'I knew someone would eventually manage to get through your defences. I knew it!' Alice stopped dancing for a moment. 'You don't need to tell me anything about him,' she added airily. 'If you've decided to give him a chance, then he must be perfect.'

Evie just shook her head. Alice's mood was temptingly infectious, if you could forget for a few seconds where they were and how much trouble they were in. Of all the things they could be talking about, this wasn't one of them. For starters, she hadn't heard Alice's story yet. Evie held up her hands.

'Later. Right now, you need to tell me exactly what is going on.'

Alice seemed to deflate in front of her eyes and Evie felt a stab of guilt which she quickly pushed aside; they couldn't afford to deal with that right now. They had to face up to the reality of their situation and work out just how they were going to get out of it. Alice sat back down and opened her mouth to speak just as the key turned in the door. Evie could feel her breath catch and she looked at Alice — who seemed, for the first time since Evie's arrival, a little scared.

'They said they wouldn't hurt you.' Alice's words come out in a rush. 'I did what they asked.' Alice looked worried now. 'It's just painting. It's not like I'm hurting anyone.' She looked desperate for her sister's approval, and Evie flashbacked to when Alice was a little girl.

'It's okay, Alice. It's okay. Just do what they ask. We'll figure this out.'

The door swung open and two men, dressed in suits and looking menacing, stepped into the room.

'You come with me.'

But they weren't pointing at Alice. They were pointing at Evie.

26

Evie got slowly to her feet, trying to work out what was going on.

'You said she could stay here with me.' Alice's voice wobbled with emotion.

Evie kept her eyes focused on the two men whose faces gave nothing away.

'It's okay, Alice,' she said, forcing her voice to remain steady even though her insides were churning. 'I'll be fine. I'm sure I'll be back soon.'

Alice reached out for Evie's hand — whether to try and hold her back or to convey a message, Evie wasn't sure. One of the men stepped forward, and although his face was blank, it was clear to Evie that she had a choice: she could either walk or be dragged. Not wanting to leave her sister with that last image, Evie nodded and moved towards the door.

The door slammed behind her and Evie tried not to jump at the noise. She was led, with one man in front of her and one behind, along the corridor and up a flight of worn stone steps. When she reached the top, Evie felt as if she had stepped into another world. The floor was highly polished marble and the walls were lined with artwork in heavily gilded frames. The corridor was filled with carvings and busts resting on tall display tables. It was an art lover's idea of paradise. The doors leading off of the corridor were double height, heavy oak and firmly closed. There were no clues as to where she was, and the only light came from the floor-to-ceiling picture window at the end of the corridor whose view was of expansive gardens filled with blooming plants and trees.

Evie was so engrossed in taking in her surroundings that when the heavy-set man who was leading stopped, she nearly walked in to him. The man behind reached out a hand for her shoulder and pulled her to a halt. Without needing to use words, his gaze told her firmly to wait, and so she did, knowing that any other action would likely be pointless since she could see no way to escape — and knowing full well that even if she did, she would never leave Alice. The heavyset man knocked on the door and waited. Evie couldn't discern any sound from within, but he moved forward, pushed open both of the double doors, and indicated that Evie should step into the room beyond.

'Ms Spencer, please sit down.'

Evie's eyes found a tall man, casually dressed in a white linen shirt and jeans. She blinked, as he was not what she was expecting. Somehow her mind had conjured up a much older man, dressed in a heavy, dark suit and probably with a cigar in his mouth. Clearly the mob had moved on from their representation in the movies. He was younger than she had expected, probably only a few years older than her. This room seemed to more accurately reflect his personality than the other parts of the house she had seen. It was full of technology: a massive TV hung on the wall, and electronic pads here and there suggested that everything in the room could be controlled by the touch of a button.

The room was also set up for comfort. There were two large, deep sofas, and the speaker was sat on one of them with his legs resting on the long glass coffee table. In one hand he held a latte in a glass mug, and in the other a mobile phone.

'Please, sit.' His English was excellent, as was his accent, which gave only a hint that he was in fact Italian.

Evie did as she was told. She sat on the edge of the sofa but still had difficulty with her feet reaching the floor. The man just looked at her and smiled. Evie frowned; none of this had been what she was expecting.

'Please make yourself comfortable. The seating arrangements encourage lounging.'

Evie shuffled back and realised that the only thing to do with her legs, which now stretched uncomfortably away from the floor, was either to curl them up underneath her or follow her host's example. She did the latter as she tried to make sense of all this new information.

'Firstly, I must apologise for the methods used to bring you to my home.'

Evie said nothing. What she needed now was to know exactly what was going on, and it seemed unlikely she would have anything to contribute to that conversation.

'I would not usually treat a lady so indecorously.'

Now Evie raised an eyebrow, wondering if he thought kidnapping was somehow ever decorous. To her surprise, she thought his cheeks coloured just a little.

'I have already apologised to your sister,' he added as if that somehow made it all okay.

'You kidnapped her,' Evie said, forcing all the anger and fear she had felt into her voice so he was in no doubt of her views.

'An extreme measure but necessary, I assure you.'

Evie rolled her eyes; she couldn't help herself.

'When I tell you why, I hope you will understand.' He leaned forward now in a way that made Evie feel he needed her to listen. Part of her wanted to laugh — this whole thing was getting more ridiculous by the minute — but instead she settled for a shrug.

'You love your sister, yes?' he asked, and Evie could feel his eyes carefully studying her face. She opened her mouth to speak but he waved her words away. 'That is evident by your actions, Ms Spencer. What you need to know is that I also love mine. She is the only family I have.'

Evie nodded to show that she was listening.

'My sister and her fiancé have been

taken — held to ransom, if you will — by old enemies.' He shook his head at the thought of them. 'I have been working to legitimise our business. To make it something I can be proud of.'

Evie must have looked incredulous.

'That part, I don't expect you to understand. But there are others who have different ideas. Men who would use me as a puppet for their own gain. Men who believe I have more money than I do.'

'You look pretty well off to me,' Evie said. 'And I don't see what this has to do with me or my sister.'

'Even if I sold everything I had, it would not be enough to meet their demands. And believe me, I would do it, for her. But it was not money that they wanted, but . . . '

'Fake paintings, I know that bit,' Evie said, suddenly wanting to hurry him along. 'Why didn't you go to the police?'

'The men of whom I speak are powerful. They have a long reach, and my family does not have the best history with the police. Those that are corrupted hate me for my attempts to legitimise; and those who are not, do not trust me. I cannot risk my sister's life on such uncertainties.'

Evie took a moment to digest this information. However much she hated to admit it, it did have a ring of truth from what Tom had told her.

'So instead you kidnapped my sister and forced her to paint forgeries for you under the threat of hurting her or me?' Evie's eyes flashed with anger now. If he were truly trying to legitimise, it seemed unlikely he would respond negatively to her anger. It was a risky test, and Evie couldn't help but imagine that she would be in more danger if he were lying.

'We took your sister, yes. I know that it was a frightening experience for you both, but you have my word that she has not been harmed in any way.'

Evie let out a sharp bark of laughter that contained no humour.

'And you kidnapped me because . . . ?' Evie remembered Tom's words that they wanted her so that they could threaten Alice and make her do what they wanted.

'To keep you safe.'

Evie stared and then laughed.

'Ms Spencer, there are many factors at play here. Your sister became aware of them and was concerned for your safety. We had hoped to keep you out of this until it was over, but it became apparent that would not be possible, and so I sent my men to find you.'

Now Evie was sure she was dreaming. This was all so far-fetched, and she felt certain she couldn't believe a word the man was saying. Her mind seemed to be trying to tell her something, something about what he had just said. She closed her eyes briefly, to cut out the distractions and try and allow her mind to replay the words.

'We,' she said out loud. 'Who's *we*?'

'That would be me,' an all-too-familiar voice sounded from the other side of the room.

27

Evie twisted in her seat as best she could. She had recognised the voice but somehow needed to see the person to believe it. In the corner of the room stood Ms Elizabeth Sullivan, Deputy Consul for the British Embassy in Rome, and junior only to the Ambassador. Evie's brain tried to work out if she had been there all along or if she had managed to somehow sneak in without Evie noticing. Ms Sullivan was immaculately dressed in a dark suit jacket with pencil skirt and a white silk blouse. She looked as she had that first time Evie had met her, but now there was something different about her.

'Ms Sullivan, why don't you come and take a seat?' the man asked, seemingly unbothered by her sudden appearance. 'Since this affects you too.'

Evie stared as Ms Sullivan strode

over. Despite her high heels, she managed it quickly. But instead of sitting, she stood next to the man's sofa and crossed her arms.

'Was this really necessary, Patrizio?'

Ms Sullivan seemed happy to ignore her, and so Evie studied her closely. She looked the same, except a little drawn: there were tight spidery lines around her eyes which suggested she had been frowning a lot. Tom had been right, Sullivan was a traitor. Evie clenched her fists in her lap.

'What have you done with Tom?' Evie demanded.

Ms Sullivan turned slowly to look at her and merely raised an eyebrow.

'A question you should be asking yourself, Ms Spencer.'

Evie felt as if she had been slapped. It was a fear she had carried with her, deep down. She knew that if anything happened to Tom, it would be her fault; she had dragged him into it, after all. Even if he had initially been following orders, anything he did now she knew was because he cared about her.

'Your friend is quite safe,' Patrizio said, holding up a hand and glancing at Sullivan. 'We have not harmed him in any way. I have already explained that I do not wish to go down that route.'

'And you've just told me you would do anything to get your sister back.'

Patrizio seemed to be weighing her up.

'This is true, but you have my word that I have done nothing to you friend.'

'Then where is he?' snapped Evie, wishing she was standing like Sullivan as it was hard to get across your anger when you were slumped in a comfy chair.

Patrizio shrugged. 'That, I do not know.' He turned his attention to Ms Sullivan.

'Elizabet?' he asked, his accent heavy on the word.

Evie saw a flash of anger.

'I told you. I tasked him to keep Ms Spencer 'safe'.' She said the word as if she had mimed two quotation marks.

275

'To keep her out of our way. Clearly he has failed,' she added, looking knowingly at Evie, who could feel herself start to blush at the implication.

'But it seemed he was right about you,' Evie said, forcing her voice to remain cool. 'You are a traitor.'

Now it was Ms Sullivan's turn to look as if she had been slapped. Colour started at her neck and rose slowly, taking away some of the paleness that Evie had noted earlier.

'I would never . . . ' Ms Sullivan began, and took a step towards Evie. What she intended to do, Evie never found out as Patrizio was on his feet with what seemed like practiced ease. Evie doubted that she could stand up from that sofa so gracefully.

'Elizabet, please. This helps no one.'

He turned back to Evie. 'My sister's fiancé is Ms Sullivan's son.'

The colour drained from Ms Sullivan's face and she turned white as a ghost. Patrizio strode towards one of the chairs and pulled it behind her.

With a hand, he got her to sit down. Evie blinked, trying to take in this latest bombshell.

'It is of course not widely known.'

'Does Tom know?' Evie asked.

'Of course not,' Ms Sullivan snapped, back to form so quickly that Evie moved back in her seat involuntarily. 'No one knows outside this room.' She glared briefly at Patrizio, but he merely shrugged it off.

'It was time.'

Evie thought for a moment.

'It seems unlikely that your secret was as safe as you supposed,' Evie said quietly, giving voice to her thoughts.

'Indeed,' said Patrizio, which told Evie that they had come to the same conclusion. 'Their plan, it seems, will not work without some international assistance.'

Evie nodded as another piece of the puzzle fell into place.

'So what do you need from me?' Evie asked. She said it quietly, but knew she had the full attention of both of them.

Clearly they had not been expecting her to say those words, and it gave her a small sense of satisfaction that she had figured out part of their plan before they had shared it with her. She watched as they exchanged glances. In truth, Evie had no idea what they wanted; but she knew they had taken a risk bringing her here, so that had to be something, and she doubted Alice's concern alone would have been enough.

Patrizio looked slightly uncomfortable and walked away from her before turning back to face her.

'You said you told Alice,' Evie continued, 'so I'm assuming that she has agreed to create the forgeries for you without the need for any duress.'

This did nothing to ease Patrizio's obvious discomfort, but Evie didn't really care. She had been frantic for weeks, looking for Alice; he deserved at least to feel a small portion of how she had felt. Then the sensible part of her brain reminded her that he *did* feel as she did, since his sister had also been taken.

Evie looked at the floor, feeling a cross between embarrassment at her words and anger that he had made her feel embarrassed.

'Ms Spencer, I have no right to ask anything of you.'

Ms Sullivan snorted and started to pace. Evie ignored her and focused on Patrizio. It was true he had no right to ask her, not after everything that she and Alice had been through, but then a thought struck her. Evie knew deep down that in her most desperate moments she would have done anything to have Alice safely back with her. If their roles had been reversed, would she have done the same?

'What do you need?' Evie asked, hoping that it wasn't anything illegal or worse.

'We need you to find De Santis and keep him from ruining everything!' Even Ms Sullivan appeared surprised by her outburst.

'He is getting close to discovering part of the truth,' Patrizio said, his tone softer than Sullivan's but still urgent. 'His behaviour suggests he knows of Elizabet's involvement but not her motives.' He turned his gaze on Evie and she knew that her face had probably just confirmed his suspicions without the need for her to agree or deny. Patrizio nodded slowly and Sullivan continued to pace.

'I believe he also knows that it is I who has Alice?'

Evie shrugged. That, she didn't know for sure, as Tom had never spoken of the identity of Alice's kidnappers.

'We need to provide these men with one more painting. Your sister is working on this now. We need perhaps two more days. Then we can make the final transfer, and my sister and Ms Sullivan's son will be released.'

Evie tried to swallow down the words, but she knew she had to say them out loud.

'How do you know you can trust these men? How do you know they will do as they say?'

She had to say it even though she saw the flinches of pain on both faces. If the men refused to give Patrizio back his sister — or, worse, harmed her in any way — Evie knew that would not be good for her or Alice. Whilst she thought she believed what he had said, she had no idea what this stranger would do if he was pushed that far.

'They made a vow. They will not break it, as long as I do what they ask.'

Evie looked doubtful.

'That is the way of things with old families.' Patrizio said the words as if this were fact, but Evie couldn't bring herself to buy into his hope. She turned her attention to Ms Sullivan, who had stopped pacing.

'When the transfer is complete, I will systematically dismantle their operation, with my bare hands if necessary.'

28

The sentence sounded so odd coming from Ms Sullivan's mouth, like she was reading a script from a bad movie, but one look at her face told Evie that she meant every word. And in truth she couldn't blame her for those feelings. She had felt the same about the previously unknown people who had taken Alice away from her, and she didn't have anything like the power that Ms Sullivan had.

'Okay,' Evie said looking from one to the other. 'How do I keep Tom away from all this?'

'He has some people he can trust. He is planning to uncover Ms Sullivan's actions and then come for Alice — and, I suspect now, for you.' Patrizio indicated her and Evie knew that it had been a risk to take her off the street, that it would only have made Tom more determined to come for her. It was another small nugget that made her feel Patrizio was telling her the truth.

'We need you to go to him and tell him all that you know. We feel he will believe you.'

Evie felt a pang of concern. She wasn't so sure.

'Perhaps, if I can take Alice with me. Between us we might be able to convince him.'

'Alice must stay here,' Sullivan said, in a voice that suggested no argument could dissuade her. 'Or were you not listening? Alice must complete the last painting.'

'I'm aware of that,' Evie said, forcing herself to not rise to Sullivan's insinuation that she was stupid or something. 'I'm merely suggesting that Alice leave with me for a short time to speak to Tom. After that, as long as she is happy to do so, she can return here to finish the work.'

Evie held her breath. Whilst she believed what she had been told, she in no way believed that if it came to it that they would keep Alice safe. If she could get Alice out of this place, then they could decide between them what they should do next — maybe go to the Ambassador's wife for help. Help not just for them, but for Sullivan and Patrizio too.

'No!' Sullivan said. 'It's too risky. They have us under surveillance. They know every move we make. If you take Alice, they will know. They will think we are reneging on the deal.'

Sullivan turned her full attention to Patrizio, and Evie watched as a silent conversation flowed between them.

'I'm afraid Elizabet is right. Alice must remain here. I give you my word that she will be under my protection.'

Evie clenched her fists in frustration. She knew it had been a long shot, but still she had hoped.

'Okay, but I want to see her before I go.'

'No,' Sullivan said, and her voice had returned to the disinterested calm of their first meeting. 'If you want to see Alice again, then you need to convince De Santis.'

Evie swallowed down the lump in her throat at the clear threat in those words. She turned to Patrizio, hoping for reassurance, but she found none. He held her gaze, and she could see both determination and desperation in the eyes that looked back at her.

'It is just two more days, Ms Spencer. Then Alice will be returned to you, I will have my beloved sister back, and Ms Sullivan her son. Ms Sullivan can then deal with the perpetrators, and we can all go back to our lives as they were.'

Evie moved to the edge of the sofa and stood. Her experiences over the last few weeks told her that Patrizio's prediction of the outcome was about as likely as it was that she would win the Lottery — which she never played.

'Please tell Alice that I will be back for her soon,' Evie said, and Patrizio nodded.

'My men will take you back to the

centre. You must find De Santis and convince him.'

Now it was Evie's turn to wave his words away. It wasn't as if she needed to be told what was at stake; she had been living with that fear for weeks. When another suited man entered the room and indicated that she should follow, Evie didn't hesitate. She knew what she needed to do. It wasn't just Patrizio's sister and Sullivan's son's lives on the line, she knew that it was Alice's too. Evie needed the last painting swap to work as much as they did. The doubts that the others could be trusted surfaced again, but she pushed them down; there was nothing that she could do about that, and so instead she focused on her next task — how she was going to find Tom.

The black SUV with heavily tinted windows pulled up at the kerb. The man in the passenger seat climbed out and opened Evie's door. She slid out of the car and thought she would need a moment to work out her surroundings, but to her left stood the art gallery where this had all started. She had been racking her brains as to where she might find Tom. She had considered his apartment, the shop where his cousin, Valentina worked, and even the Embassy. She still had the Ambassador's wife as a possible safe contact, but Evie was sure that an ex-M15 operative wouldn't think Patrizio's plan was a good one, and that would be bad for Alice.

She walked up the low steps that led hundreds of locals and tourists to the main foyer of the gallery, and found a quiet spot off to one side where she could sit and think. Evie knew she couldn't just sit there all day, but right now it seemed as reasonable an option as any other.

She wasn't sure how long she had sat there before one of the side doors was flung open and she heard running foot-steps. Evie twisted round to see, more curious than concerned, and saw Roberto running towards her. Evie got to her feet. Whatever else had happened, Roberto had still betrayed her, betrayed Alice.

She felt her fists clench, and part of her brain wondered if she would actually strike out at him in anger.

Roberto had obviously read her expression as his steps faltered with uncertainty. He held up both hands as if that would pacify her.

'Please, I know you are angry, but you must come with me.' His accent seemed heavier, and Evie figured it was a sign of stress.

'I don't think so,' she replied, raising an eyebrow.

'I am sorry about before. I will explain, but not here. Please. I have someone who needs to speak with you.'

'That's what you said last time.' Evie's hands found her hips.

'It is not safe.'

Evie said nothing, and then frowned as Roberto seemed distracted by something — by what, she couldn't tell. She stared at his face as his eyes looked off and to the left. She turned but couldn't see anything. Turning her gaze back to his face, she could see a thin tell-tale wire looped around his ear. Evie took a step back. Roberto couldn't be from Patrizio, he would have told her, which only left one option: the people who had kidnapped Patrizio's sister. Evie started to scan for escape routes, tensing her muscles ready to run.

'He says he needs you by his side so he can keep an eye on you,' Roberto said. Evie stopped and stared. 'He says you were right. He should have taken you with him, it was the only way to keep any eye on you.'

Evie's mind didn't have to work hard to remember the conversation she had had with Tom. A conversation no one else could have overheard, especially not Roberto.

'He also says, 'Please don't be a wildcat'.' Roberto frowned and shrugged as if the words meant nothing to him — but they meant everything to Evie, and it could all be summed up in one word: Tom.

Roberto took one step back in the direction had he had come, held out a hand, and Evie fell into step behind him. They didn't go back into the gallery, but instead walked down the narrow alley at the side of the huge building. Here there were large bins on wheels and wooden crates which had been emptied of their wares. Roberto weaved a path between them and Evie followed, her mind conjuring up an image of Tom: his eyes, his smile, and the feeling of being held by someone she truly trusted.

Roberto paused and Evie wondered if he were listening for messages again. He nodded, but for whose benefit she wasn't sure, and headed off to the left. Evie was starting to get impatient, and felt the tiniest niggle of worry that perhaps she was being betrayed one again. She slowed her steps as she tried to work out what to do, and then two hands grabbed her from behind.

29

Had it happened minutes before, Evie would not have been ready; but her distrust had been woken inside her, and she was ready now — ready to fight and ready to run. As the arms surrounded her, she forced herself to relax, to lull her attacker into a false sense that she had given up. And then she twisted, suddenly and violently, but it was of no use. It was as if the attacker had anticipated her actions.

'Steady there, drop the wildcat act.'

Evie knew that voice, would have known it anywhere, and all the fight left her. In fact, her knees felt as if they had turned to jelly, and she wondered if they would fold and take her to the floor. Tom must have thought the same, and she found herself lifted up into his arms.

'It's okay,' he said softly, 'I've got

you. You're safe now.'

Evie buried her head in to his chest and felt him kiss her lightly on the head. With her eyes firmly closed, she focused only on the sensation of being carried and feeling safe. She knew they were moving, but to where she didn't know — and if she was honest, she didn't care.

The change in lighting told her they were now indoors. Tom lowered her and Evie knew that he was planning to put her down, so like a child she tightened her hold around his neck, not ready to let go yet. Without words he turned and sat himself, holding her tightly on his lap.

'Roberto, some water, please?' Tom said.

Evie frowned a little; she couldn't work out what Roberto was doing there.

'He betrayed us.' She murmured the words and then forced herself to sit up a little; this was too important for her to cling onto being weak and feeble.

'Not exactly,' Tom said as he rubbed her back. 'They found him and threatened Alice if he didn't help them find you. It may not have been the best choice, but from his perspective at the time, it was the only choice.'

Evie felt a little anger bubbling up inside her. It was alright for Tom — he wasn't the one who'd been kidnapped off the street!

'My burning question right now is, how did you escape?'

The question distracted Evie from her anger. Yet again, the sensible part of her brain reminded her that in Roberto's place she might have done the same, and that was without considering the fact that it had probably all worked out. *Probably*, her heart reminded her; they weren't at the end yet.

'I didn't escape. They let me go.' Evie wriggled a little so that she could see Tom's face. If she had any chance of convincing him, she needed to see what he was thinking. Tom was looking at her with barely concealed disbelief.

'Why did they bother taking you in the first place? If it wasn't to threaten Alice with harm to you . . . ' His voice trailed off as he seemed lost in thought, trying to compute this latest piece of information.

'Well,' Evie said slowly, knowing she needed to choose her words carefully, 'I guess, to get a message to you.'

Tom's expression hardened and Evie knew that he was beating himself up. Their feelings for each other were the reason she was taken. She held up her hands.

'No, it's not like that.'

Tom raised an eyebrow.

'I need you to listen to me, really listen. Please?'

Tom took a moment and then nodded slowly. Evie stood up — with a great sense of reluctance, but she knew she couldn't convince him if she was curled up in his lap — and told him everything she knew.

'And you believe them?' Tom asked, his face carefully neutral, but Evie was used to seeing through that.

Evie shrugged, feeling a little help-less.

'I'm not sure we have a choice. If Patrizio is right, then anything we do might put all of them in danger, including Alice.'

Tom stood up and started to pace, running a hand through his hair, and Roberto looked on, completely lost for words.

'You picked a hell of a time to start trusting people, Evie,' he said, and then seemed to realise that he had said the words out loud.

Evie wanted to tell him that would be entirely his fault, but held her tongue.

'Could it be true?' she asked, going for a reasonable tone. 'I mean, is Patrizio trying to grow a legitimate business?'

Roberto let out a laugh that was full of bitterness.

'His family history would tell us otherwise.'

Evie glanced at him and then back to Tom. It was Tom after all that she needed to convince. He was right, of course — she had picked a ridiculous time to start trusting strangers — but something deep within her was telling her that the best way to keep Alice safe was to do as she had been instructed.

'It's possible, anything's possible. Patrizio definitely has a sister, and if he were trying to go legit, she would be the most effective target.'

'Did you know Sullivan had a son?' Evie asked. Tom shook his head.

'No, but in her position I would probably have kept a lid on that too.'

Tom paced and Evie let him. She knew it was a lot to process.

'Why did she not tell you?' Roberto demanded, breaking the silence. 'You are her second-in-command, no? What if this is a trap? If it is, Alice will never be released. What if the other family, whoever they are, decide that they want to keep her?'

Evie's blood ran cold. How had she not considered that? Alice's art was a commodity, but surely an artist who could keep producing work would be a better option. The fatigue and fear seemed to well up again, and she felt for the chair behind her and sat down. With her eyes tightly closed, she felt someone take a seat beside her.

'Take some slow, deep breaths,' the voice said and she knew it was Tom. She shook her head; they didn't have time for her to do this right now.

'No,' she said, managing to squeeze the words out. 'Alice,' was all she could manage before she felt another surge of the shakes. A hand gently pushed her down and lifted her feet up to rest on the chair.

'We need to consider all the factors before we make a decision. A few minutes' rest and some water and food will not change anything, Evie.' His words were comforting, his presence was comforting, but not enough to push down the fear and uncertainty. Had she made a terrible mistake in believing Patrizio and Sullivan? As the minutes ticked by, her mind raced — but what else could she have done? It wasn't as if she could have single-handedly broken free and escape what was obviously a well-guarded home.

Evie swallowed one last time and went to sit up. A hand held her back but she gently brushed it away. Tom studied her, then handed her a bottle of cold water, which Evie drank hungrily, realising just how thirsty she was. She then took the offered chocolate bar and felt the sugar start to revive her.

'Do you trust them?' Tom said softly, sat at her side and watching her closely. Roberto made a noise, but with one look Tom silenced him.

'My gut feeling is yes,' Evie said, shaking her head as she saw Tom's expression. 'But we can't take that as fact! What if I'm wrong? You've already both come up with risks I hadn't even considered!'

She felt his hand rest on hers. 'Evie, you've said it yourself — you don't trust anyone.' He smiled a little as if to remind her that he was one of her few exceptions; she rolled her eyes, but she couldn't help the small smile that escaped. Roberto shuffled his feet, but they both ignored him. 'I would say, with your experiences, you are the best person to decide whether a person is trustworthy, since your natural default is to not trust anyone.'

'I trusted Roberto, and look where that got me.'

Roberto opened his mouth to protest, but Tom got there first.

'You said yourself that you would do anything to protect Alice. Is it unreasonable to expect the same from someone else who loves her?'

Evie fidgeted. Tom's reasonableness was getting annoying.

'So we're just going to sit here for two days and wait for Patrizio, the head of one of the most notorious crime families in Italy, to keep his word and release Alice to us?' Roberto was shouting, but his face said the emotion was nearly fear.

'No,' Tom said firmly. 'We're going to

monitor the situation and take action if we need to.'

'How?' Evie asked.

'Patrizio is well-known for conducting business at his property. Where he feels safest and has the upper hand at all times. From your description, it sounds as if that is where Alice is being held — so we will do as they ask and stay out of it, but that doesn't mean we can't be close by and keep watch.'

'But what if they see us?' At first the plan had seemed so logical and reasonable, but now all Evie could feel was fear.

Tom turned to her and smiled.

'So all of a sudden you trust the head of a notorious crime family, but not me?' He was trying to lighten the mood, but Evie could see the tightness round his eyes.

'I haven't slept properly for weeks. I've been kidnapped and jumped out of windows. I'm not sure that we should trust *me*,' Evie said, almost pleading.

'I trust you,' Tom said. 'Sometimes in

an apparent no-win situation you just have to decide to trust something — or, in this case, someone.'

'But what if I'm wrong?' Evie said, and the shaking started again, but this time it was accompanied by tears.

'I promised you we would get Alice back, and we will.' Tom said the words with such certainty, but it didn't quell her deep-set fear. Then Evie was pulled back into his arms, and it felt like she was home.

30

Tom had been busy and Roberto had been following his orders. Roberto, having seen that Tom would not be moved on the plan, had obviously decided that it was the only way he could be involved in bringing Alice home. Evie, for her part, had slept. At first she had point-blank refused; but her body, exhausted and beyond sleep, had finally made it clear that she was going nowhere. Tom had reassured her that he would not leave her behind, and so she had given in to it all and slept, curled up on the sofa with a blanket over her, cold despite the warm day.

She was glad later that she had slept — she felt slightly more herself — but now she was awake, the seconds seemed to drag by, and she felt as if all her nerves were on edge. Finally, when the sun had set on the following day, Tom announced that they needed to move to the spot where they could monitor the exchange. Evie had expected that they would be camped out in some utilities van, as they always did in the movies; but instead she and Tom ended up in a high-end apartment block which gave them a clear view of the rear of an exquisitely expensive complex of residential buildings.

'How do you know this is where it will happen?' Evie asked as they settled in with high-power binoculars and a camera with a telephoto lens.

'People like Patrizio are creatures of habit. It is how they survive. I doubt very much he will veer from that for someone as precious as his sister.' Tom kept his eyes focused out of the window, but reached over to squeeze her hand.

Evie's mind wandered to Alice and the room she was being held in. She had processed much at the time, and it was not exactly a prison: well-furnished, and with all the mod cons that Alice could want, save for perhaps a view of the outside and the ability to actually leave. Evie couldn't help but think about how Alice might be feeling. She veered from relief that it might soon be over, to the deep-seated fear that something could go terribly wrong which seemed to be eating away at her insides.

'Are you awake?' Tom's voice drifted across the darkness.

'Do you see something?' Evie ignored the suggestion that she could have fallen asleep; her brain kept running through all the things that could possibly go wrong, and wasn't about to give her a moment's peace even to shut her eyes.

'There's movement, but I think it's just prep work.'

Evie scooted across the floor so that she was by his side, but so that her movements couldn't be seen by anyone looking in.

'When do you think . . . ?'

Evie didn't get to finish the question as the street below them was suddenly bathed in flashes of bright lights. Tom was on his feet and running for the door. He grabbed something on his way past the small table, and Evie's heart clenched as she realised it was a gun. He was taking the stairs two at a time before Evie had even reached the door. She followed him — even though he was shouting for her to stay put, she ignored him.

As Evie stepped off the last stair there was a further flash of light that hurt her eyes. Despite furious blinking, it seemed it had temporarily blinded her. Accompanied by the ringing in her ears, she couldn't make sense of what was up and what was down. She reached out her arms, trying to feel for something which would provide her with reference, but found nothing.

'Get down!' a voice commanded. It was English with no trace of an accent, but she knew in an instant it wasn't Tom's. Hands grabbed her and pulled her, and as her senses started to return, she found that was now sheltered by the broad staircase that ran up to the first floor.

'Stay here,' the voice said, and Evie was so close to the stranger that she could hear the hiss of the radio in his ear.

'Copy,' he said, and then Evie felt that he was gone. She pulled her knees up and wrapped her arms around herself as she felt someone else fall beside her. She reached out a hand, wondering if it were friend or foe. There was something familiar about his presence.

'Roberto?' she asked

'Alice,' he groaned. All anger and resentment now forgotten, Evie threw her arm around his shoulders.

'Tom will find her,' she whispered, over and over again, the only thing keeping her from losing it completely.

As her hearing returned, Evie could make out what the noises were. There were no more pops and bangs, but still shouting.

'I cannot stay here,' Roberto moaned, and pulled himself to his feet. Unsteadily, he weaved to the door, and Evie followed him. Right now, the only thing she could do for Alice was to keep safe the man her sister loved.

Roberto scrabbled to find the door handle and pushed. He was outside, with Evie beside him, and they both stopped, trying to make sense of the scene before them. There were cars everywhere, mainly black and new. A few police vehicles were parked at angles with their lights still flashing. Someone — Evie could only presume it had been the good guys — had set up powerful floodlights so that they street was bathed in light. Men in all-black combat gear stood to attention around vans, as people in suits and police uniform were shepherded inside. There was no sign of Alice, Tom, or Patrizio.

'My sister? Tom De Santis? Have you seen them?' Evie asked the first man in black they came to. He looked at her and shrugged, and started talking in Italian. It was clear from his gestures alone that he wanted them to leave the area, and that it was not just a suggestion. Roberto stepped forward and quickly started to translate Evie's original question. The man pointed in the direction of what looked like a mobile command centre.

'He doesn't know, but says the British Embassy staff are based in there.'

They made their way towards the command centre. It was slow going as they were repeatedly stopped and asked for identification. Each person who stopped them checked first on the radio before ushering them forward. The door to the command centre was closed, and when they knocked it was opened by Ms Sullivan.

'I won't waste my breath asking how you managed to be here,' she said, but Evie's close study of her face told her that whatever had happened it was over and had all gone to plan — hers, at least.

'Alice?' Evie asked, her throat so tight that her words could barely fight their way free.

'They're bringing her out now.' Sullivan said.

'And the . . . others?' Evie asked not sure whether she should mention that one of the others was in fact Sullivan's son.

'My son is safe. He has been taken with his fiancé to the hospital to get checked over.'

Evie's face must have flashed concern.

'Just a few cuts and bruises, nothing serious.'

A woman in a suit stepped forward and murmured into Sullivan's ears.

'You might want to step outside,' Sullivan said, and a smile seemed to be tugging at the woman's lips.

Evie turned to leave, her mind focused on the two most important people in her life, but her hand was grabbed and squeezed. Sullivan opened her mouth to speak but did not seem able to find the right words. Evie nodded; she recognised the sentiment, at least, and in that moment had no words either. Sullivan let go of her hand and gestured that she should leave.

Evie reached the bottom step as two figures appeared between the tall, pillared gates to the property. Evie would know them anywhere, even though they were in deep shadow. Tom had an arm thrown protectively around Alice's shoulder, but Alice seemed none the worse for her ordeal.

Roberto ran forward and swept Alice into his arms. He spun her round on the spot, and Evie's heart fluttered at the sound of Alice's laughter. Then Evie's eyes sought Tom out. The man who had promised to bring Alice back to her; and who, despite the odds, had managed it. Without realising it, her feet were starting to move, and despite the lack of sleep she was running and running; then she felt his arms encircle her and she could hear his heart beating in his chest.

'Thank you,' Evie managed to say between the sobs of relief that had started, unbidden to wrack her body.

'No need,' Tom whispered into her hair. 'I don't doubt that you would have found a way without my help. You are one determined wildcat.'

Evie found a giggle build in her chest, mixing now with the sobs. If someone had called her a wildcat three weeks ago, she would have simply stared in disbelief — caution had always been the name of the game until now.

'It's all because of you,' she said, and then stood on tiptoes and kissed him. Everything around them seemed to fade away, and something inside of Evie seemed finally free.

'I don't want to interrupt or anything, but it would be nice to get some sisterly love.'

Both Tom and Evie giggled, kissed gently once more, and then broke apart. Within a heartbeat, Alice's arms were round Evie's neck.

'I love you,' Alice said.

'I love you too,' Evie said relief filling every part of her.

'He's not hard on the eye, either.'

Evie held her sister at arms' length and glared, but it was a half-hearted effort.

Tom stepped forward.

'We haven't been formally introduced, I'm Tom De Santis. Your sister's . . . '

Alice cut him off. 'Boyfriend? Or have you moved on faster than that? Who knows what you could have got up to whilst I've been indisposed? I don't know, I leave you alone for three weeks, and you go and find the man of your dreams.'

Tom put his arm around Evie's shoulders and she leaned in. She looked up into his eyes and she saw the question there. What were they to each other?

'More than that,' Evie said softly; and Tom nodded, a grin spreading across his face.

'Well, I don't know about you two lovebirds, but Roberto and I have decided that what we need right now is some wine. Scratch that: lots of wine, and then maybe some food.'

'I know a great little place,' Tom said.

'Will it be open?' Alice asked as

Roberto stood behind her with his arms around her waist. He looked completely different now, and Evie realised with a start that he seemed whole.

'Don't worry, I know the owner,' Tom said, and reached out for Evie's hand. They walked away from the scene hand-in-hand, with Alice and Roberto talking animatedly behind them.

'So,' Tom said, 'will it be my place or yours?'

Evie looked up at him and frowned.

'I'm not sure I can wait to travel to mine to get a glass of wine.'

Tom smirked.

'I didn't mean now. I meant later. Since I have no plans to let you out of my sight ever again, I was just wondering where we would be living.'

Evie blinked. It was not what she had expected him to say — wanted, yes; but expected, no. A small warning voice told her they were moving too fast, but with ease she swiped it away. Her new found instincts told her everything about being with Tom felt right.

She glanced over her shoulder to Alice and Roberto, who were looking deeply into each other's eyes, a wordless confirmation of love passing between them.

'Yours,' Evie said

Tom looked surprised.

'Are you sure?'

Evie nodded.

'My home was for the old me. I'm not that person anymore, and I don't want to be. I want to be with the people I love, with you and with Alice.'

Tom stopped and pulled her into his arms. His kiss this time was deeper and more urgent.

'I love you, Evie Spencer. Stay with me forever.'

Evie gazed up at him.

'On one condition.'

'Anything.' He lifted a hand and ran it through her hair.

'Marry me?' Evie said.

Tom blinked and was clearly surprised. He opened his mouth to speak, but no words came.

'The ultimate sign of trust?' he asked, looking both relieved and excited. Evie couldn't speak, so simply nodded. She had never imagined saying those words, never imagined trusting a man enough to accept them, let alone offer them herself. But she knew that he understood that. They had known each other less than a month, but he understood her better than anyone else, and she loved him for it.

'Yes, Evelyn Spencer. I would be honoured.'

And then, as if she were in any doubt of his intentions, he pulled her into his arms and kissed her in a way that she couldn't help thinking was probably best left to the bedroom, before she smiled to herself and relaxed to enjoy the moment.

We do hope that you have enjoyed reading this large print book.

Did you know that all of our titles are available for purchase?

We publish a wide range of high quality large print books including:
Romances, Mysteries, Classics
General Fiction
Non Fiction and Westerns

Special interest titles available in large print are:
The Little Oxford Dictionary
Music Book, Song Book
Hymn Book, Service Book

Also available from us courtesy of Oxford University Press:
Young Readers' Dictionary
(large print edition)
Young Readers' Thesaurus
(large print edition)

For further information or a free brochure, please contact us at:
Ulverscroft Large Print Books Ltd.,
The Green, Bradgate Road, Anstey,
Leicester, LE7 7FU, England.
Tel: (00 44) **0116 236 4325**
Fax: (00 44) **0116 234 0205**

LOVE WILL FIND A WAY

Miranda Barnes

Convalescing after a car accident, Gwen Yorke leases a remote cottage on the beautiful Isle of Skye. She hopes to find inspiration there for her career as a rug designer, and wants to decide if she and her boyfriend have a future together. In Glenbrittle, she finds herself drawn to the enigmatic, moody Andrew McIver, and his young daughter Fiona. To Gwen's delight, she and Fiona become close, frequently sketching together. But why is Andrew so unhappy about their friendship?

THE PRINCE'S BRIDE

Sophie Weston

One of three royal brothers in the Adriatic principality of San Michele, Prince Jonas works hard. But after a protocol-ridden evening, he's due some downtime in his beloved forest. Hope Kennard was the daughter of the manor back in England. But she has guarded her heart since her childhood ended in financial scandal. She's just passing through San Michele, before moving on to another country, another job. But then a charming forest ranger appears. And this time, her instincts don't help . . .

THE UNEXPECTED GIFT

Sarah Purdue

When London nurse Megan Falstaff is informed she's received an inheritance from her beloved godmother Cathleen, she's expecting a couple of cat figurines. What she actually inherits is a boarding cattery in the village of Little River — with the stipulation that she must run it for at least a year. Getting to grips with the eccentricities of felines and village folk alike is challenging for Megan — and matters aren't helped by the disdain of the haughty vet Doctor William Wakefield . . .

ONLY TRUE IN FAIRY TALES

Christine Stovell

Eloise Blake has been fascinated by Prospect House, the shadowy romantic Gothic edifice opposite hers, ever since she moved to the village of Hookfield. When its new owner turns out to be bestselling crime author Ross Farrell, whose work is grounded in gritty reality rather than happy endings, she is determined to concentrate on her tapestry design business and her rescue dog Gracie. Love, she thinks, is only true in fairy tales. But is Ross the Prince Charming she thought didn't exist — or is he a beast in disguise?

THE MAGIC CHARM

Christina Green

When Goldie Smith spies the portrait of the three Crosby girls for the first time, belonging to her dear Great-aunt Mary and painted long ago by an enigmatic local artist, she can't help but wonder at the history behind it. She also takes an instant shine to Rob Tyson, the handsome man who comes to photograph the painting. But his first love seems to be the rare birds he makes extensive trips to record with his camera. Is there room for Goldie in his life as well?

YOU'RE THE ONE THAT I WANT

Angela Britnell

When Sarah, a teacher from Cornwall, and Matt, a businessman from Nashville, meet on a European coach tour, they soon find themselves in a relationship — a fake one. Because Matt is too bust for romance, and Sarah is only trying to make her ex-husband jealous. For every picturesque destination, there's a loved-up selfie and Facebook post to match. But as their holiday comes to an end, Sarah and Matt realise they're not happy with their pretend relationship. They want the real thing . . .

FINDING ALICE

Evie Spencer has always lived life cautiously, wary of trusting anyone other than her beloved younger sister Alice, a talented painter who is studying art in Rome. Then Alice suddenly disappears — and Evie, determined to find her, must throw caution to the winds. Inexplicably stymied by the British Embassy, Evie is frustrated and desperate . . . until the mysterious Tom De Santis offers assistance. But there is more to him than meets the eye. Can Evie trust him, and succeed in finding Alice?